MW01044979

Simon Says

"The role of a writer is not to say what we all can say, but what we are unable to say."

- Anais Niin

Simon Says

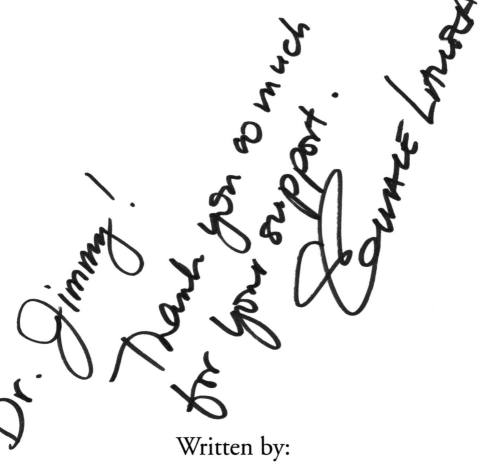

Dr. Jimmy!

Thank you so much
for your support.

Dawnie Laroza

Written by:

Dawn Grace Laroza

To order additional copies of this book, contact:
Xlibris Corporation
1-888-795-4274
www.Xlibris.com
Orders@Xlibris.com
81903

Foreword

Simon Says . . . Hello!

A world of diversity needs stories that reflect the nature of human existence. Too often literature is written about a small segment of the population and therefore reflects only a tiny fraction of human experiences. Stories that attempt, in any way, to redress the imbalance, to tell new stories, to illuminate more of the soul and spirit of human kind—are welcome. Simon Says is a book that is rich in diversity and attempts to tell a big story about the lives that we live.

I grew up in a world where everyone was white, everyone spoke English. Where no one was disabled, no one was very much different than me. In that world of my childhood, television told stories about people who looked like me, spoke like me and had aspirations similar to my own. In the land of fiction there was no poverty, there was no hunger, there was no prejudice. Everything always worked out in the end. We all dove into fiction to escape our realities for the realities of those very much like ourselves.

And yet there were whispers.

Private whispers.

In my own family there were secrets not told, stories not told, lives lived in shadows. My mother's cousin, Mattie, I only heard about in conversations cut short when I entered the room. She was shrouded in mist and mystery. She lived, vibrantly, in my imagination. All I knew was that she was never there. That she never came to family gatherings. That she was the ghost in the room that no one spoke of but that everyone felt.

As I got older I began to ask question about who this girl was. I wanted to know. My questions were brushed aside, as much with anger as with embarrassment. I was being 'protected' I know, but I didn't know what I needed protection from. I thought that she might have had some horrible disease – in those days the word 'cancer' was never spoken aloud. But, no, she didn't have a disease. She had something considered much worse. She had a disability. She had Down Syndrome.

I never did learn her story. No one ever told me. Even though I entered the field of disability. Even though I became a wheelchair user. Even though I was desperate to know. No one ever told me. My family couldn't shake the shame of silence, ever. I think perhaps the source of shame has changed. With time and understanding those who had kept the secret have realized that the shame was never her disability but, rather, our treatment of her. Shunning someone, for the crime of difference, is an incredible act of violence.

It is because of Mattie, that I appreciate writers like Grace Laroza as she bravely tackles new territory. By creating a story wherein difference, all human difference, is openly discussed, she makes it possible to imagine a world where new stories will be told. Stories that welcome into breath, those of whom we, at one time condemned to silence. Ours. And theirs.

-Dave Hingsburger
Director of Clinical and Educational Services
Vita Community Living Services/
Mens Sana Families for Mental Health

Writing my first novel has always been a dream of mine and a promise I made to my Mom. But I never would have been able to write one without the love, help, support and encouragement of the following people. Thank you:

Dad—Thank you so much for always supporting me and my dreams. Remember what I said: Just always have a good heart and Mom will always be proud of you.

Kenner—The first 6 years of my life meant nothing until you were born. Not only did I gain brother, but a best friend, and at times my worst enemy (Jerk). Thank you for being there always. You know I'll always be there to support your dreams too. Just make sure you know your place in the biological timeline.

Ace & Elsie Laroza: Team Laroza is all about family. Thank you both for being part of our team.

JC—I formulated my idea for Simon when I saw how wonderful of a father you are to Jacob. So proud of all you have done and continue to do, J—and you know that I'm always here for you. Thank you for always being there for me. Love you bro.

To the Leandelar family: I can't forget you. I won't forget you guys. I wouldn't have been able to write this without you in spirit. Thank you.

Claire Miranda—CB, Growing up, I never really had a friend who I could turn to. I was always the black sheep. When I met you in 2000, I had no idea I would not only learn the true meaning of friendship, but also what it means to have a sister. You have no idea how much your love, friendship and support means to me. If I could give you the world, I would. Love to Jay and JJ too. You guys are family to me.

Lisa Miron Rambaldini: Having you as a part of my family has been the best thing to ever happen to us. Lisa, you have always been my guru; someone I have always looked up to. You may be our family lawyer, but you're also family. You were brought to us, and the best way possible. Thank you for your support always.

Gilda Raimondi: Gil you always tell me to never let anyone put me down and to always go for my dreams. Thank you so much for always encouraging me, for being brutally honest with me and for never letting me down. You always tell me to follow my heart. Your words is what got me through this book. I guess that's what it feels like to have an older sister.

Ivana Rodic: Even after the darkest of nights, there is always a light. That light is you. Friends forever. Thank you so much for everything.

Folashade Akanabi: Best part about Japan? You.

Dr. Arne Kislenko: Arne, when I get discouraged, I put my "Arne-face" on. It only takes half a second to work! Your friendship throughout the last decade has been on of my most precious gifts. From the day I met you, running around in your classroom making one of the most boring topics in the world so interesting, I found not only faith in teachers/professors, but also a life long friend. I can't thank you enough for being there for me throughout all these years. Years go by, but you always find time for me. You once told me that there isn't anything I couldn't do. Best advice I ever got.

Faysal Ghandour: Fays, either it's camera lessons or designing the cover of my book, you have been such a great support throughout the process. Your encouragement is phenomenal. It meant so much. Thank you.

Kirk DeMatas: For being my muse. And the epitome of strength. Keep on doing what you do and I'll be there to support you no matter what.

To Bob Rumball Center for the Deaf especially Christine Coffey, Lisa Faria, Phillip Daniels. Thank you for helping me write from a different view and perspective. Thank you all so much.

And of course, to those who I inspired my characters, those who helped shaped my characters, those who cheered me on when I got discouraged, those who pushed me from Day ONE, helped me through the entire writing process and of course the gift of friendship: *Dave Hingsburger, Nicholas Walker, Rachel Upson, Allyson Glass, Quinn VanAntwerp, Jeff Madden, Aimee Granger Husic, Shelley Devereaux, Emma Rockett, Andrea Corbo, Ileana Font—Soloway, Sharon N'Diaye, Pete Bryan, Danielle Ruel, The Jadraque family, Anca Barbuc, Nicola Hengst, Frances Fong-Lee, Emily Lyons, Nicole, Norma and Steven Palacios, Nathalie Mercur—Europa, Mohamed Mhmmoudi, Khadija Channouf, David G. Williams, Lydia Tsang, Nam Chuong, Grace Lisboa, Naoko (Just in case) Inoue, Yoshimi Yamada, Kim and Yasmeen Bishop, Sanaa Siddiqi, Glenn Calderon, Kevin Ali, Roxanne Speers, Stephanie and Jedd Sybingco, Suzanne Manickam and O, Elyssa Carroll Goldman, Nancy J. Carroll, Theresa Tapas, Monica Maartinik, Lynn Berger Heyne, Kim Loiselle, Zorana Alimpic, Zico Ramnarine, Tiffany Cumming, Erin O'Brien, Alexis (Roomie) Mapes, Sasha*

Romanowsky, Susan Toombs, Tyler (TBaby/Tila) York, Makafui Amenuvor, Caity (Roomie) Robinson, The Morissey family, Darah Aljourdar, Emma Titley, Jeff Edmunds, Alayne Sampson, Wayland James Sermons, Jasmine Purdie, Grayson M. Posey, Gracie Y., Melissa Huerer, Alan Glass, Andrew Levy, Tom Kingston, Nick Barjaktarovich, Julius Agawin, Geric Agawin, Valerie Ventura Agawin, Taylor Ventura Agawin, Connor Ventura Agwain, Jacob Otzkaratay-Agwain, all my amazing coworkers and my girl, Skye. Thank you.

To all the people I have had the pleasure of supporting in the disabilities field; to past, present and future Cross-Cultural Solutions volunteers and CCS staff worldwide, and to my mom, Nelia Leandelar Laroza (1952- 2003).

Mom, this one's for you.

Chapter 1

My name is Simon. Before we go to further introductions, I better tell you right now. I'm deaf. I don't realize it when I scream. I was born deaf and my biological mother gave me up for adoption before she even found out my gender. Do I sound bitter? Nah. My adoptive parents were always open about this and told me right away that I was adopted when I was old enough to understand. So there is no hiding whatsoever.

My parents are my heroes. We have always been close. They told me that they tried years to have children, and it wasn't possible. They told this to me when I was a mere five-year-old and finally asked what "the birds and the bees" had to do with sex. My parents, bless their souls, had no idea that they were going to adopt a child who was deaf from the get-go, so when they found out, they immediately started taking classes at the community center down the street and learning everything they could about sign language.

However, anyone can tell you that learning a completely different language in your midthirties or forties—when English is not your first language—is difficult. So we communicated with games. My whole life has been a mixture of sign language, notepads, drawings, charades, dry erase boards, and notes. I cannot properly sign, and I never want to learn how to properly sign. Upon observation, I had learned to read people's lips. In fact, I got so good that I insisted that every night during dinner, my parents had to talk to me with their mouths full.

"That's bad manners, Simon," Mom signed.

"That's a great idea!" Dad signed. Dad won.

One summer, my parents and I went to improv workshops. My sign language with my mother is slightly different than my sign language with my father. Something as slight as being right-handed and left-handed can throw off their conversations. I've learned to deal. My father is a cartoonist and has drawn pictures for me my entire life. I, of course, learned the proper way to sign when I went to school. I signed proper sign language while at school but reverted back to how my parents signed when I was at home. It made me feel like we were part of some special club—a club that only the three of us knew.

My parents had a social worker work with them each week when I was adopted, and this social worker had told them that I needed to go to day care for the deaf and learn sign language immediately. Apparently, that didn't go too well with my headstrong parents, because they never called her back.

When I was nine years old, my mother announced she was pregnant. That always confused me. My father tried to draw me a whole comic strip and showed me a couple of videos, but I got even more confused. It was only when I got older that I find out that whatever you believe in, some higher power works in mysterious ways. On my tenth birthday, I celebrated my special day in the hospital, welcoming my new baby sister.

My sister, Emma, was perfect in every way. She had my mother's Ghanaian-colored skin, which was tinted lighter by my father's Costa Rican complexion. Emma had a flat, button nose, wide-set eyes, and small stubby fingers. The doctor told us that she had a "mild case" of Down syndrome. I had no idea what that was, but to me she was perfect in every way. I never knew that Emma was different than anyone. How could I have known? I'm different too.

My parents were beside themselves with joy at a baby girl in the house. The odds were against them, apparently, since my mother was nearing forty-seven when she had Emma while my dad was thirty-six. Having a baby sister was a huge change. As much as I was happy to have a little person to boss around, I was very jealous of my sister. My entire life, it was me and my parents only, and I always had the attention of my parents. Now I had to share this with my new baby sister.

I wanted to know when Emma was crying, so my father had my room installed with lights that flickered every time Emma cried. Unfortunately, Emma was a very fussy baby and was colicky. The lights in my room flickered all the time, giving off the impression that we had a never-ending lightning storm, so I ended up sleeping under my bed. I was terrified of lightning, always have been, ever since we got caught in a horrible lightning storm once. So I slept under the bed, because I couldn't see the lights switch on and off. I remembered the look of relief on my mother's face three weeks after the lights were installed in my room. She had crouched down and was staring at me. She had no idea that I was sleeping under the bed and thought I was missing. They called me, but of course, I couldn't hear.

"We looked everywhere for you," Dad signed while my mom cradled me in her arms. I laid my head on her heart and listened to the rapid beating to calm down my nerves. The sound of a mother's beating heart is music to anyone's ears.

"I have been sleeping under the bed for the last two weeks," I signed back. Mom and Dad looked at each other. "You only noticed now?"

If Mom blushed, I couldn't see it, but with Dad, he turned a deep shade of red. I grinned inside. The next day, Dad spent the entire morning with me. He called me his special helper, and we mowed the lawn together. Then we went biking together. Mom stayed back with Emma, and then they switched. Dad took care of Emma while Mom and I baked sugar cookies. I watched closely as Mom measured the flour.

"Do you and Daddy love me as much as you love Emma?" I signed. Mom looked at me, her beautiful Ghanaian features now twisted with shock. I repeated my sign. I had to know. I looked at her dead in the eye. I knew how much my parents hated when I did that, when I tried to intimidate them with my eyes. It was a skill I learned early on. I could stare right at them and not blink. Dad is terrible at it. He would blink after three seconds. Mom, she mastered two seconds more than Dad.

When I was younger, I would sit in front of the mirror and wait to see how long it would take for me to blink. My longest was seventeen minutes. My shortest was eight minutes and thirty-five seconds. If I can't use my ears, I can most definitely use my eyes, right?

Mom put down the measuring cup and looked like she was trying to brace herself. Call me observant.

"I guess you were eventually going to ask me a question like this," Mom signed, her smile so full of love. The way Mom smiled always made my heart stop. Her whole face lit up. She didn't necessarily smile, she more like grinned. And then her whole face lights up. I waited.

"There is no 'more' or 'less' in this family," Mom signed carefully. She brushed the flour off her hands and then wiped them on a wet dishtowel on the counter. "I know you feel that because you were adopted and Emma was not adopted that we would love her more than we love you."

I nodded attentively. Watching Mom sign was always so funny. She mixes up her words, and she talks while she signs. Her face scrunches up when she is trying to stress a specific word. Dad said she looked like she was constipated. I was trying hard to not laugh because I sensed the seriousness of the conversation. A conversation that I started. Poker face.

"You're as much our child as Emma is, and we love you both the same," Mom signed.

I grinned up at her. "Really?"

"Of course."

"Well, I already knew that," I signed back.

I didn't, but I wanted her to know that I did. Mom made a face at me. "Then why did you ask?" I stuck my tongue out at her and reached over for the spoon that had the sugar cookie dough.

"To hear you say it," I signed. Mmm. Sugar cookies. Mom hit me on the head with her spoon. I didn't even hear it coming. Ha. Get it?

Chapter 2

I'm a big brother. So it goes without saying that when you're a big brother, you protect your younger siblings. I have always protected Emma. Yes, I had jealousy toward her and sometimes even hatred—mainly because she was different from me in many aspects. She was my parents' biological child. I know that my parents have always said that I was theirs and that they chose me—but it is hard to separate that. Emma looked like them. I did not. I had strong Arabic features, green eyes, and unruly hair. I have no idea who my own biological parents are, and at this point in my life, I don't want to find out. I dreamed about it a lot when I was a child. One day meeting my biological parents. How they would go down on one knee with arms wide open, ready to catch a running me into their arms.

Then I would daydream about how angry I would be at them for giving me up for adoption. I have a very vivid imagination so I can picture clearly how angry I would be, what I would sign, and even kick my father in his shin. I would imagine the big black bruise with my name on it. I could see their faces so clearly when they realized I couldn't speak and their frustration when they saw that they couldn't communicate to me. And how terrible they would feel when they realized that they missed out.

Then I would daydream that as much as they wanted me back, they couldn't have me back because I had the best adoptive parents in the world. Who loved me despite my disability. I daydreamed about my biological parents all the time. I knew nothing of them. I would ask my mom some questions and sometimes my dad. My dad never wanted to talk about my adoption. He would get upset and retreat into his study.

The first time I asked my dad about my biological parents, he got flustered. I asked again and got angry. I had learned early on that getting angry gives me the answers I want. Pounding the table with my fists always got them going. I remember the hurt look in his eyes for even asking. Finally, he stood up and left the kitchen and retreated into his study. He didn't slam the door; he shut it quietly, eyeing me with downcast eyes before shutting the door completely. I ran toward the door to open it, but it wouldn't budge. He had locked the door on me. I didn't see him for the rest of the night. Dad slept in his study that night, and I slept on the floor in front of the study. I took comfort in knowing that my father was hurt that I had asked, as sadistic as it sounded.

I woke up the next morning on my bed. I had my pajamas on, and my mouth slightly tasted of toothpaste. I ran my tongue over the left side of my mouth. A glob of toothpaste was resting there. I went downstairs. Mom was in the kitchen, squeezing oranges. She looked up when I came into the kitchen and smiled slightly. She looked tired.

"Good morning, Simon," Mom signed. I looked around the kitchen. Emma was sitting on her high chair, fixated on three Cheerios on her high chair table.

"Where's Dad?" I signed back. Mom emptied the orange juice into a pitcher before signing back.

"He left early." I waited for her to tell me where, but part of me didn't want to know. I felt terrible. You could see it in my mother's face that she was hurt too. I walked over to Emma and planted a kiss on her head. Her dark brown eyes grinned up at me. Mom was watching us. I went over to my seat and saw that there was a folded piece of paper on my plate. Out of the corner of my eye, I saw that Mom was waiting for me to see it before she turned her back toward the sink.

I sat down and opened the piece of paper slowly. Inside was a family drawing. A caricature of us. Mom with her perfect back posture, carrying Emma placed on her hip. Dad was standing behind me with his arm around my neck, us tilting slightly as if caught by the wind. We had these huge grins on our faces. Dad had also drawn a huge heart around the entire family.

"Dad drew this?" I signed. Mom was watching me. Mom nodded.

"Why is he so angry?" I asked. "I just wanted to know."

Mom pursed her lips and picked up a dry erase marker. She went over to the dry erase board and wrote, "Dad is afraid that you want to know because you want to find them when you're older." As an afterthought, she added, "I am too."

"What is wrong if I wanted to find them, though?" I signed. It was a bold question. I never did want to find them, but part of me was thinking that they were part of some FBI conspiracy, or I was really a prince . . .

Mom looked like I had slapped her in the face. Emma gurgled. I sat down next to her and kissed her on the top of her head.

"Do you want to find them?" Mom asked carefully. I shook my head.

"I just want to know if they're really cool . . . like they're part of the FBI or the king or queen of some foreign land . . . ," I signed truthfully. I ignored Mom's hurt look. She had no reason to be hurt. I loved this family and I loved my parents. There was no way I would ever leave them. Mom sighed. "Simon, I'd rather talk to you about this with Dad around. He should be part of this conversation." I shrugged.

"I have to go to school," I signed.

"You have half an hour before the bus comes. You need to eat breakfast first," Mom wrote on the board. She turned her back toward me and went back to squeezing orange juice. I helped myself to a bowl of Cheerios. I dipped my hand into the box and grabbed a handful. I counted out seventeen cheerios. Well, seventeen and a half. One was half. I put the half on Emma's bowl who grabbed at it immediately. My hand went back inside the box and grabbed another handful out. I counted out six more Cheerios and dumped the rest back on Emma's bowl. I couldn't eat Cheerios with milk as it would make the Cheerios soggy. I poured a glass of milk carefully and then took a sip. One sip to one Cheerio. Mom turned around.

"Si, you have ten minutes," Mom signed impatiently. I hate being rushed. I drank the last of my milk and saw that I still had thirteen cheerios left. Uh oh. I grabbed one and threw it into my mouth. I missed. I watched it fall to the floor and glanced up at Mom. She wasn't watching. I kicked it under the kitchen table. It's okay. Twelve is unlucky too. I picked up another one and threw it into my mouth. Eleven is okay. Eleven is a good number.

I dug into my bag and pulled out a crayon. On Dad's drawing I wrote, "Love you too, Dad," right over the picture of him and me. I left it under his ashtray turned candy holder. Mom saw me and grinned. She blew me a kiss and signed, "Have a good day. See you at 3:30 p.m." I grabbed my lunch from the counter and ran out. The bus driver, Kimmie, was flashing his lights. He waved at me then looked up and waved at Mom, who was watching from the doorway with Emma in her arms. I ran into the bus, grinning. I sat in my usual spot. Opposite Kimmie so he can sign to me when he drives and picks everyone up.

"Hi, Simon," Kimmie signed. "How many Cheerios were left over today?"

"Only eleven, sir," I signed back, smiling. Only eleven.

"Is that a good number?" he asked as he turned the key on the ignition.

Kimmie knew it was. "Very." A good number means a good day.

Chapter 3

For someone who is deaf and mute, you would think that I had a tough time going to school. For some reason though, being deaf and mute had its advantages. One thing, I couldn't hear the teasing, if there ever was one. I barely made eye contact until I felt it was safe to do so. Mom reprimanded me on that one evening when we went out for dinner with a couple of Dad's coworkers. I was so shy and couldn't look up. Especially when I met Dad's coworker's beautiful daughter. She was very tall, at least a head taller than me, had curly dark blonde hair, light hazel eyes with brown specks in them, and a cute smile. When Dad's coworker said, "Call him Uncle Nick. Short for Nicola." "I'm Italian," Nick said proudly to Dad, who thought Dad was going to translate this to me. Dad didn't bother.

Dad signed to me upon Uncle Nicola's insistence that I be introduced to Nathalie, Nat for short. I was spellbound. Nat, when she found out that I was deaf and mute, quickly ran into her room and got out a small old Etch-a-Sketch and beckoned me to come over to her. She quickly jotted down. "My parents wanted me to give this to Goodwill, but I didn't want to. I knew that I would have a reason . . . (*shake shake shake*) . . . to use it! :-)"

I was in love. And said so to Mom a few weeks later while we were playing Scrabble. Dad had learned a new English word that involved a V, B, and G, and he wanted to see if he could use it in the game to finally get out of third place. I knew Mom would relay the message to Dad about my crush. "Is that why you barely looked up from your meal?" Dad signed, with a grin. I nodded, my face flushing. Unfortunately, with my dark complexion, you can't see my blush, but my parents and sometimes even Emma knew when I was blushing. Emma would smile at me slyly if she noticed I turned a darker shade of Moroccan.

"Your eyes, as cheesy as this sounds, are what a woman looks into," Mom wrote this down on the board. Dad made a big show of rolling his eyes, then bugging them out, then blinking them rapidly. I laughed. Mom ignored him.

"Your beautiful eyes, so green, so intense, you should never be ashamed to look into someone's eyes. Especially someone you have an interest in." I saw Dad laugh. Then he signed to Mom. "We need to talk normally with Simon if we're going to get through to him. We can't say, 'Someone you have an interest in.' You might as well say, 'Someone you are courting.'" Dad shuddered while Mom laughed.

Dad turned to me. "Look at a girl in the eye when you have the hots for her. She'll fall in love with your green eyes." Mom made a look of protest then resigned. "Yes, she will," she signed back to me. "Be proud of who you are." Mom continued. "I know that you sometimes feel like you have a disadvantage, but trust me—there are a lot of men, boys, teenage boys out there, who can fully talk and hear, but 90 percent of the time have nothing to say or don't listen."

Dad nodded vigorously when Mom looked at Dad for support on this sexist statement. When she turned back to me, Dad shook his head, waved his hands, pointed to his chest, and gave me the thumbs-up.

"I will arrange another dinner with Fred and his family," Dad signed. "I don't know much about Nathalie, just that she's a very sweet girl, has asthma, and loves math." I turned up my nose. "She loves math?" I signed.

Dad shrugged. "Apparently."

"Good, Si, if you end up getting married, she can do our taxes." Mom winked.

I thought of Nathalie all the time. Especially before I went to bed. That's when Mom and Dad finally decided to have the talk with me. And change my bedsheets to plastic ones. All of a sudden, I was finding "what to do when you hit puberty" pamphlets in my room. Dad came home one day with a blue square CD. Boyz II Men.

"I know it's a music CD, but I didn't know it was until I bought it. I thought it was a documentary with subtitles. I'll find out if there's a karaoke version. They're pretty good," Dad signed. I laughed until my stomach started to hurt. Dad became a huge fan and got Mom hooked, and they both went to a concert few years later.

Mom was responsible for the pamphlets. I tested her. I threw one in the garbage once, and it was her week to clear out the trash. The next day, I found exactly the same pamphlet on my pillow. Stuck with a safety pin on the corner so it is easy to read without opening it. I pricked my hand a few years ago and hated safety pins. The irony.

Nathalie and I didn't go to the same school. I found out she was two years older than I was. That meant she was fourteen. I didn't know where she hung out or whom she was friends with, but I asked Dad about her every day. Dad reported on her every evening. Mom looked at Dad in exasperation. "Does Nick ever wonder why you ask about his daughter every day? Did you tell him about Simon's crush?" Dad shook his head. "I mention it casually, 'Simon asked how Nathalie is doing,' and he just brags about her like a proud father would. I do the same."

"When are we having dinner with them again? Or why don't you invite them here?" I asked. "They would love to meet Emma." Emma had stayed with a babysitter the night we went over to Uncle Fred's.

"Next Sunday, we're going over there and I'll invite them over here after."

The following Sunday, I burnt my finger on the iron. While Mom was putting some medicinal ointment and wrapping it up with white gauze, she laughed at me. "You don't iron jeans, Simon." I was annoyed. They were my favorite pair of black jeans, and it had taken me nearly all morning to find them. I found them rumpled in the corner of Emma's room. She had used it as a cape. I couldn't get mad, so I left her room and decided to iron for the first time. The iron barely touched the jeans when I yelped in pain. Mom heard me and ran to pull the iron out of the socket.

"Dressing to impress?" Mom signed. I laughed and nodded. "Wear a genuine smile. That always gets us girls."

When Uncle Nick and his wife, Melfy, opened they door, they explained that Nat had gone to church. I couldn't hide my face. Melfy caught my expression and tried to explain to Mom that the church was having a small rehearsal for a concert they were having and that I could go and meet Nathalie if I wanted. It was within walking distance.

"I'll walk you there," Dad signed to me. "Where is the church?" After a hasty drawing of a map, Mom took Emma inside to meet Uncle Nick and Melfy while Dad walked me to the church.

"What if I'm bothering her?" I asked. Dad looked at me. "Well, they're rehearsing, but I'm sure she'll be happy to see you. I'll stay with you for a bit until she sees you. Don't be worried."

"What kind of church is this?" I asked as we rounded the corner. A beautiful stone gray church with the crucifix stood on the top of the church.

"St. Michael's Catholic Church," it read on a stained-glass billboard on the side. I stopped in my tracks. "May I go in? We're not Catholic!" I signed to Dad. Dad smiled.

"It's all right! Every church, mosque, and temple has open arms. They're like banks. Buildings don't judge. Only people do." And with that, he pulled the heavy wooden door open.

I have never stepped foot inside a Catholic church before. Mom being Muslim and Dad being Protestant, neither of my parents practiced, and on my adoption papers I was written down as "Muslim" under religion. My parents were not very religious, but they were very spiritual. Mom and Dad constantly talked about God when I was growing up, and it was through this that I learned that God was with us always. In fact, Dad even had a tattoo. "Thank God," in his inner left wrist. "Just a friendly reminder," he told us. He also had a crucifix tattooed on his chest and two hands praying on his right forearm.

Mom was not a practicing Muslim, but she had learned to sign "*Masha'Allah*" and "*Insha'Allah*" and incorporate it into conversations with us. "*As-Salamu Alaykum*" was also a common sign that Mom learned. Dad and I learned to reply. "*Wa'alaykum salaam*." A few years ago, Mom and Dad took Emma and me back to Morocco for a two-week vacation. "It is important for you to see your roots," Dad signed. I was excited. I wanted to show Emma where I was adopted, and the palm trees that I remember so vividly in my dreams. I was not even a year old when I left Morocco and was nine when we went back. I was surprised when I saw that the orphanage had closed down. "Did you know?" I asked Mom. Mom nodded. "They sent us a letter a few years ago, and there was a nurse who worked with you a lot. She had sent baby pictures of you with her." She pulled it out of her wallet. Emma grabbed at it.

"What happened to her?" I studied the picture. She was very pretty, with long dark-brown hair, and dressed in patterned cloth pants and a dark blue V-neck shirt. Her mouth wasn't smiling, but her eyes were. I could see my face . . . one eye was opened. I laughed. "Me?" Emma asked, pointing to the picture. "Si?" Dad nodded. "Spitting image," he said, winking at me.

"We're not sure. I was hoping to find out. It's not a big deal though. She had said that the orphanage was relocating because there was something wrong with the plumbing, but she didn't mention where they were relocating to." Mom wrote this all down on a notepad. I nodded. I didn't care to see the nurse. It was nice to see the picture, and I was happy it was sent to my parents, but I had no desire to see any nurses. I took Emma's stroller and walked her over to the gates of the orphanage. Mom and Dad followed, Dad kicking broken pieces of shard glass out of the way.

"This is where Mom and Dad adopted me, Em," I signed to Emma. Emma had no idea what I signed, so Dad translated. Emma looked like she didn't care. She stared through the gates for a second. "Simon, since we're here, do you want to go to a mosque?" Mom signed.

Dad smiled with encouragement. It didn't feel right. No. I shook my head. Mom nodded.

"That's all right, Simon. We just thought you would be interested to see what a mosque looked like. Later on, the *azan* will go on. One of the most beautiful sounds ever. It's the call of prayer. You won't be able to hear if, but if you want to see everyone praying, let us know."

I shook my head again. "Do you want to go, Mom?" I signed. Mom shook her head. I knew that Mom was Muslim and sometimes felt bad for not being a practicing Muslim. Especially during Ramadan. Dad always said he'd fast with her if she wanted to fast, but Mom always said no. Her explanation was simple. "I'm Muslim by name only. One of my sisters—she lives in Accra now—she's a Christian. When I was born, my parents claimed I was Muslim. When my sister was born a year later, they claimed she was Christian. That's how it is in Ghana." She smiled.

"Doesn't that defeat the purpose?" I signed as we walked away from the orphanage. I didn't bother to look back. We stood off to the side and waited for a taxi.

"Sai, it's all a matter of perception," Dad signed. Mom was already pulling out the notebook and a pen for this talk. "Mom's family lived in a village where Islam and Christianity are very open and accepted. In fact, that's how it is like in Ghana. I remember when I went to visit with Mom, there was a sign on a store that said, 'Allah wants to you come in!' and right next to it was store with a sign that said, 'Jesus loves you! This much!'" I laughed. "I have traveled far and wide, Simon, and I have to say that Ghana was the friendliest country I have ever been in," Dad finished. Mom looked at Dad with eyes of affection. She pulled his arm down and kissed him on the cheek.

"The friendliest country?" I signed incredulously.

"Of course! Everyone smiles at you, there is no such thing an outcast in Ghana, everyone is so happy to see you. When they were there, they called your dad '*we-vu*' because he's white. It means white person. Trust me, though, they say 'we-vu' for everyone who is a different color. I remember an Asian volunteer from Canada coming to volunteer in nearby school where I worked once and the poor girl was running away from a group of kids yelling. "We-vu! We-vu!" But it's a sign of affection. By the end of that week, she had stopped running from them.

"Ghanaians all know . . . at the end of the day, it's the same God who gave us this wonderful life. Unfortunately, its people's idea of religion that ruins God's best gift. That's why people fight. Religion is such a touchy subject with people, but that's where the pride and ego come in. It's really sad," Mom signed. "When we have money, Sai, we will go. We will make a trip to Ghana and Costa Rica."

"*!Pura vida!*" Dad signed. Another phrase that Mom and Dad learned to spell in sign language. I laughed, remembering how to sign "!Pura vida!"

"'!Pura vida! It's a pure life in Costa Rica!' *Ticos* say it all the time. In passing, in greeting, *all the time*!" Dad signed to me. Dad spelled it, then showed me the "!Pura Vida!" tattoo he had tattooed on his rib cage. "There's an upside-down exclamation mark before the pura and then a right-side-up exclamation mark after the 'vida.'"

"So, Sai, this is how we're going to say !pura vida!" to each other. We can spell it in sign language, but this is better" Mom stood up from the kitchen table to demonstrate with a grin. Dad was so excited, he looked like he was about to explode. She put both hands together as if to pray and gently smacked my right cheek with it. Then, she crossed her eyes and wiggled her tongue while she shook both hands from aside her face, put her hands back in prayer and smacked the other side of my cheek. I squealed with delight. I did it back to Mom, and then to Dad. Dad did it back to me then Dad pumped his fist in the air.

"!Pura vida!"

A taxi showed up about four minutes after Dad flagged one day. Before we went in, Dad asked in sign language to the driver. "Do you speak English?"

"*Anglais?*" the taxi driver asked. "*Non. Parlez-vous Français?*"

"Um, no . . ." Dad shook his head and we waited another five minutes to flag another taxi down.

"You guys make it so simple, religion," I commented, signing. Mom broke an airplane cookie from her purse and handed one-half to me and one to Emma.

"If it's so simple, why the fighting? Why all the animosity?" I asked. I had to sign-spell "animosity."

"Sai, every single person out there has their own idea of religion. Majority of people are born into their religion without a choice, and therefore, that is all they know. When it's all you know, you are influenced by those who surround you with the same religion. And they have learned it from their ancestors. And their ancestors. It goes way back. If you're so entwined with the religion you are born with, you tend to get superior and are not encouraged to be open-minded. There are some people out there who strongly believe that their religion is the only religion, and will go to great lengths to make sure the world knows. Thankfully though, it has changed a lot. Especially where we live. But it's still a problem," Dad signed.

"There is a huge difference between religion and spirituality, Simon. Never forget that," Mom interjected.

"How so?" I signed.

"Well Sai, This is just our opinion. I want you to feel free to ask these questions not just to us, but if you have questions at school, we want you to ask your teachers, your guidance counselor. If you have a teacher who has difficulty with sign language, write it on a piece of paper and let us know too.

"We would be more than happy to be there while you ask. You have every right to ask. If you feel that we are wrong, or our explanation is wrong, then let us know," Mom signed. Dad nodded eagerly. "Just because we're your parents, doesn't mean we know everything. Every day is a learning process. There is so much in the world to learn, and to assume that we know everything is pretty damn arrogant of us. Might as well be actively practicing a religion if that's the case."

"You can tell Mom is a bit bitter, Simon." Dad grinned, as he opened a bottle of water from his backpack and handed it to Emma. "Want one?" he asked me. I shook my head. He asked Mom and she shook her head. "I'll just drink from Emma's."

"I'm not bitter, Simon, it's just that that is why I stopped watching the news. There is always something about religion and how something went wrong and people went on a killing spree. People use the word 'religion' to their advantage and bend the rules of their religion to accommodate them. It's human nature. They figured, if they're in that religion, why not? God still loves them, or Allah or Ganesha or Buddha . . ." Dad's signing trailed off.

"Don't get me wrong, I respect all religions. Most people need order in their lives. But I have to say that there are some who are just in a religion to show off, to look like they belong somewhere, to meet people, to be a part of a team, etc. They were born into it, right? So why not? Or some people leave the religion they were born into and convert to another religion because they want to defy their parents, or look cool, some do it for love. They will wear the hijabs, or avoid pork, or have meatless Fridays, or pray the rosary, or go vegetarian. They will go to mass on Sunday or church on Sunday, go to the mosque on Fridays or fly to Tibet and learn to meditate. I think it's so beautiful when people genuinely want to learn about another religion, but some convert for the wrong reasons. It's all a catch-22." My favorite book.

"If it is," I signed, "then why bother?"

"To belong," Mom signed simply. "But that's where the whole difference between religion and spirituality come in."

Dad flagged down a taxi with an English-speaking driver and we all hopped in. Dad jumped into the front seat after folding Emma's stroller into the backseat. Dad indicated us to head to our hotel. Mom continued.

"Everyone wants to belong so badly to a religion, unless they are atheist and claim to not believe in God. That too, is like a proclamation of your identity. Maybe they went through hardships in life, and did not grow into a family who enforced religion. They claim that their life is so bad that there must not be a God, or where is God when there is so much suffering in the world? So people get upset and refuse to believe there is a God, when it is so evident that he is there, and it is us alone who refuse him into our lives." Mom paused as she was talking so passionately that her eyes started to water from the side. Dad turned around halfway and tried to grab Emma's hand. Emma reached out.

"The thing most people don't realize, or never seem to, or maybe even refuse to, is that you don't have to be part of an organized religion to believe in God. That, Sai, is the difference between religion and spirituality, in your father's opinion and mine." Our taxi reached the front of our hotel. We were going to rest and then go to the *souk* before dinner. With Dad pushing Emma into the hotel, Mom continued with her explanation of religion and spirituality. I was thoroughly enjoying this conversation. One thing, Mom had gained a lot of confidence with her sign language. She had given up trying to jot down all she wanted to say and just went with the flow. I understood every single word she was trying to tell me and with reading her lips and her sign language. Dad was more confident with his ability to sign to me, but he was not as confident with writing things down.

Also, I was completely enjoying their ideas of spirituality and religion. It was true, when I was growing up, I always felt God's presence in our lives. God was always part of our conversations, Mom and Dad always mentioned him every day. How thankful we should be that we had each other, that we were healthy and that we were living in Canada, with endless opportunities. We said thanks, Christian-style before every meal, and we always did a list of thank-yous right before bed.

Emma was extra good in finding things to be thankful for. "I am thankful that it rained today so Daddy doesn't have to waste water when with the garden hose," "I am thankful that Mommy's anger toward Daddy taking the remote only lasted fifteen seconds," "I am thankful that the toilet didn't clog up when I used it after lunch today." She always ended with. "I am so thankful that I have the best brother in the world" and spent nearly a year with our parents in learning how to sign this to me.

We haven't stepped foot in a church or a mosque as a family, and during occasions such as Ramadan or Christmas, both Mom and Dad celebrated with gusto. I grew up with books about religion, and was constantly asking questions. What my parents didn't know, they bought me a book about it. Then we learned it together, discussions during dinner especially. Dad was well-informed about Christianity, and had taken a great liking to Hinduism and Buddhism, and studied books on his own. Mom learned more about Christianity, Catholicism, and Islam on her own. I think they wanted to be fully prepared when I had questions. I hardly had any questions. Once in a while, I did, but my parents were very vocal about supporting whatever religion I wanted to choose when I was older, *if* I wanted to choose an organized religion. They also stressed that it wasn't necessary, but it was my choice if I wanted to be a part of any organized religion and they would support me in every decision I make.

I was also so happy to know that they had adopted me from Morocco, and took me back to Canada with them. Despite my disabilities. Doctors found out when I arrived in Canada that I was mute after a series of tests for three years straight. There was speculation that I had autistic tendencies, was obsessive-compulsive, etc. In my mind, I was not wanted. I wasn't perfect. Yet my parents wanted me. They wanted me and did whatever they could to make sure I lived a good life.

I knew how hard they struggled financially. Coming to Morocco was an eye opener for me, even though I was too young to admit it. The heat, the people, the style, the call of prayer. Everything was so different than what I was used to back in Canada. I only had my eyes to take in the beauty. Everyone who walked by, I wondered if they were my parents, if they were my blood relatives, if they knew who I was. Although Mom and I were very close, I always knew that Dad could feel things about me before I even said anything. I was so thankful that they had taken me, and that they were so knowledgeable about life.

That night, at dinner at a French-inspired restaurant, I had an allergic reaction to couscous and Emma wouldn't eat it. I thought they would have French fries, but they didn't. I ate bread instead.

"Religion is a sensitive topic, Sai," Dad signed to me, while we lathered margarine onto slabs of fried bread. It was delicious. "So this is how we think. This is how your mother and I have come to understand religion. And as your parents, we will instill what we think into you and Emma. Who knows if we're right? Who knows if we're wrong? God is real, God has always been real. He's with us this very moment, as he is with everyone who believes in his love and his power. God only exists when you love because God is love."

"It is too bad that that is the very thing alone that causes people to fight and kill others," I signed to both my parents before I handed Emma a piece of bread slathered in margarine. Mom smiled at me sadly.

"Everyone has their own opinions. The best thing to do is just to accept people for who they are. Who are we to change things? The concept of each religion is different, but it teaches all the same things. To love one another, to respect each other, to not hurt or kill others, to be kind to each other. To let go of your ego. We, as your parents, could be completely wrong, but this is what we came to understand. God is always with you, in fact, God led us to you, Simon. He also gave us a beautiful daughter," Mom smiled over at Emma. "and gave us challenges because he knew that we could handle them. God doesn't give us what we can't handle. We are thankful that he trusts us enough to give us the cards he has dealt."

I thought back to that time in Morocco as I stood in front of the St. Michael's Church. It was a beautiful church. I spotted Nathalie at the choir, who looked over at me and squinted. Dad waved and pulled my arm so I could wave too. When she noticed who it was she smiled a flashlight grin, exclaimed. "Oh!" and came over to us. We met her halfway down the aisle of the church. I was trying to keep the stupid grin off my face; I knew it was there because my cheeks on my face started to hurt. She waved at us both, her smile so open, I could count all her teeth.

"What a surprise!" She shook Dad's hand. Dad signed, "We're having dinner at your house tonight, and Simon wanted to see you at church!"

Without her Etch-a-Sketch, Nathalie just waved again. Dad laughed and pulled out a small notepad from his jeans pocket. He opened it to see if there was anything there he had written, saw that he had and reached into another pocket. He found a fresh pad and handed it to Nathalie with a pen. Relieved, Nathalie took the notepad. She scribbled quickly. "Want to stay and watch choir? I'll be done in half an hour, and then we can walk back for dinner." I nodded eagerly when I read her note. Dad squeezed my forearm and said, "Simon has a cell phone, he just gets texts on them. But here is my wife's number just in case."

For some reason, I wasn't embarrassed. I looked up at Dad gratefully, who winked. Nathalie caught on and blushed. She grabbed my arm. "Let me introduce you to my choir mates." I had no idea what she said because she wasn't facing me so I couldn't read her lips. Suddenly she stopped in her tracks and looked at Dad and nodded, who must have bellowed. "Use your notepad!"

Nathalie introduced me to a few of her choir mates. She wrote their names down when she introduced me to them, but the church was too dim for me to put a name with the face. I remember reading the names "Andrea," " Ileana," "Ena," and "Danica." There were two beautiful twins. "Mia" and "Keanna." I also met the choir director. "Jayson." They were very friendly. Smiled when Nathalie mentioned that I couldn't hear what they were saying, but I could read lips if they spoke slowly enough. I waited for the slow, teasing, exaggerated talking, but it didn't come. I wrote on my notepad. "Pleased to meet you all, I am sorry if I can't hear you all sing."

Nathalie laughed. "Maybe you can read our lips when we sing and recognize some of the songs," she wrote. "We're getting ready for the Christmas concert already." I sat in the front pew and tried to catch some of the Christmas songs they were singing. I knew none of them. I was waiting for. "Jingle Bell Rock" (Emma's favorite!). "Rocking around the Christmas Tree" (another one of Emma's favorites!), and "Chestnuts roasting on an open fire." My parents' favorite and one of mine.

Nathalie's choir didn't sing any of these. I didn't want to admit that I didn't know what songs they were singing, but I was in awe at how in sync they all were. They looked over at me and smiled while they sang. When they were finished, I clapped my hands by shaking them off to each side of my body side. They had no idea what I was doing, so I pounded both my palms together. The choir director laughed at me. "What an audience!" He said, when he saw my enthusiastic appraisal. "Did you recognize all the songs?" Jayson spoke so fast that I couldn't read his lips. I tilted my head off to one side to show I had no idea what he said. He brushed it off with a wave of his hand and grinned.

"Thank you for coming, Simon," Nathalie wrote on the notepad and shoved it under my nose. I smiled and wrote, "No problem. But I have a confession to make. I did not recognize any of the songs you sang."

Nathalie read what I wrote. "You didn't?"

"Not at all," I wrote back. "What did you sing?" Nathalie made a few bullet points. "O Holy Night," "O Little Town of Bethlehem," "O Come All Ye Faithful," "Joy to the World."

"You didn't even recognize 'Joy to the World'?" Nathalie wrote. I shook my head. I don't think my family has ever played any of these songs at home. I mentioned as much to Nathalie. Nathalie grinned and shrugged. "You should come again to next week's practice. Maybe you will recognize the songs after next week. It would be nice if you came to the Christmas concert. It's in a month." I copied down the songs she mentioned onto my own notepad and wrote that I will tell my parents for sure.

I was not as nervous as I thought with Nathalie after that evening. Nat didn't treat my disability as a burden or as an oddity. She genuinely acted like a friend. I was flattered when she started to text me. Our friendship blossomed just as I imagined it would. Nathalie's friendship was comforting, her smile was pleasant and she was so kind to Emma. Emma took a great liking to her. My parents were happy to see I was happy. The night before Christmas Eve, she leaned forward and kissed me on our way home from choir practice. It was a small peck on my lips, but I was taken by surprise. She was taller than me, and had to bend down to kiss me.

When she pulled back, I felt like an idiot. I wasn't even expecting it, and now I couldn't cherish it. I wanted her to kiss me again. I wanted to ask, but I was blushing furiously. She smiled at me slightly. Then, she took her right mitten off her and spelled. "Seasons Greetings." I was touched. I signed it back. For the first time in my life, I had experienced a different kind of love. A love that made me sweat in places I never knew I had.

There were many questions I wanted to ask Nathalie, but I asked my parents first. I wanted to make sure I was all right in asking these questions.

"Simon, why would you ask her such a silly question?" Mom signed one evening when we were sitting in front of the television. Emma had picked *Home Alone 2: Lost in New York* as her movie preference and it was her choice that night. I thought Dad would back me up, as he usually does, but he was giving me the same weird look Mom was giving me. "Simon, that's ridiculous. You don't need to ask her why she likes you. You don't need an explanation."

"Maybe she pities me," I signed dejectedly. I was happy, floating, happiest I have ever been. Thinking about my tall girlfriend had made my heart feel lighter. But my insecurities were getting the best of me. The majority of our relationship was based on text-messaging and note-exchanging. We couldn't go to the movies unless there were subtitles and hardly any of the Hollywood blockbusters had subtitles. We ended up renting most of the time because they had that option when you put in the DVD. Emma enjoyed this because majority of the time, she spent the evening with us. There were times I didn't mind, but the evenings I wanted to kiss Nathalie, Emma would giggle at us.

"Sai, your eyes are falling out of your head," Emma signed at one point. Mom overheard and looked over at me with a smile. I looked at her desperately. Mom grinned knowingly and ushered Emma into the kitchen. "Help me wash the dishes," I think she said. She didn't bother to sign since she wasn't directing the comment at me, I only knew because Emma stomped her foot and started to cry. Dad came into the kitchen and hoisted Emma over his shoulder and gave me a wink. Mom followed suit and they all left.

Nathalie had seen the entire debacle and didn't say anything. She grinned at me and pulled out her notepad. "Valentine's Day is coming up. Want to do something special?" she asked. I shrugged. Of course I did. I just didn't know what. I pulled the pen out of her hand. "Give me something special to think about and I'll let you know," I wrote. Then as an afterthought, I wrote, "Is there anything you want me to plan?"

Nathalie shrugged and sighed. She sat back and wrote, "I don't know. There's a concert I want to go to, but I know you can't hear."

I read her face immediately. She was getting bored of me. I didn't know what to say. This was the first time Nathalie had suggested she wanted to do something but knew that I couldn't do it, and her face showed disappointment that I couldn't do it. I didn't know what to say. Part of me felt rage. I had to hide it, though. I sat back too and counted my breathing. In and out. Deep breaths. It's what my social worker taught me when I was feeling anger. Mom said I sounded like I was snoring. Nathalie didn't respond. She knew that I was upset. And she wasn't doing anything to reassure me that everything was going to be okay.

Ten minutes had passed. I glanced at my watch several times. Finally, Nathalie wrote on the notepad.

"Simon, I don't know if I am feeling this anymore," she wrote.

"Feeling what?" I wrote back.

"This." Then she started to cry. "I am so sorry. I wish you were normal," she wrote when she was able to get her shaking hands to stop long enough to write the sentence down. I had never seen Nathalie cry before. It made her look ugly. It made her look pathetic. I was seething. I snatched the pen from her. "I AM NORMAL." I wrote in block letters. "You're just too stupid to realize it," I wrote. Nathalie looked down at what I wrote and gasped.

"Did you just call me stupid?" she asked. She didn't bother to write it down, she looked directly at me, her lips quivering and I read every word she said. I nodded, defiant. How dare she not think I am normal? I am normal!

She looked at me dead in the eye and raised her right hand up. Slowly, she started to spell a word. *R, E, T, A . . .* I slapped her hand away. I stood up and pointed to the door, my hand shaking. I started pounding the wall with my hand, tears coursing down my face. I raised my foot and started kicking the coffee table with my heel. I kept slapping the wall and soon Dad came running down, with Mom and Emma in tow. I signed furiously. "She needs to leave!" to them.

Nathalie was already gathering up her stuff and pulling her jacket on. "Don't worry, I am about to leave right now," she said to my bewildered parents. Dad looked confused and flustered. He grabbed his keys from the kitchen counter. "I'll drive you home, Nathalie," he said. Nathalie just walked to the door. Dad looked at me helplessly. I crossed my arms and did everything I could think of to not let any tears fall from my eyes.

Mom let Emma's hand go and she ran to me. Emma hugged my leg, but I didn't hug back. Mom rubbed the small of Nathalie's back. Nathalie refused to turn around to me, and I didn't bother to watch her leave.

Five minutes later, the lights in the hallway flickered, indicating that the door had been shut. I sat on the couch and started to cry. Mom came over and gathered me in her arms. Emma looked so confused. In her mind, Simon never cried. I felt Mom running her hands through my bushy hair, and I wailed. "Mom, she called me the R-word and said that I was not normal! Just because I couldn't take her to some stupid concert for Valentine's Day."

Mom's eyes were livid. She was angry. "You're too good for her anyways, Sai. Don't worry." She held me in her arms and I cried the night away. Half an hour later, Dad came back home and joined us on the couch. Dad was a big hugger, which is one of my favorite things about Dad. He hugged all three of us on the couch. When my sobbing subsided I looked at Dad. "Is it going to be weird to see her dad at work?" I asked him.

"Nah, not really. He doesn't like the fact that I'm not a huge fan of his Tiramisu. After that, it was over for our friendship. We were just civil to each other because of you kids," Dad signed. I don't know why, but I thought that was the funniest thing in the world. So did Mom. Emma asked. "What is a tira . . ." She couldn't say the rest. Dad laughed. "I'll buy some at an Italian bakery tomorrow," Dad signed. "I know where they make them incredible."

I was broken-hearted for a week. I didn't eat. I only drank when my throat felt like it was like sandpaper. I moped around the house. I couldn't get over the fact that she knew how to spell the R-word so well, when she struggled to spell words like "love" or even "like." She never learned how to spell my name. Yet she knew the R-word so well. Every time I thought about it, I felt a fist clench at my heart.

I never heard from Nathalie after that night. No text, no e-mail. I didn't dare contact her. My family tried their best to get me out of my depression. We had pizza every night with pineapple (the only pizza I will eat), which my entire family hated, but which they shoved down for me because they knew I wanted them to try it.

"It's milky!" Emma wrote on the dry erase board she carried around with her all the time. I laughed. "Em, you can take off the pineapple. I won't mind," I signed to her. Emma looked fearfully at Dad. "Daddy will get mad," she signed. "We have to try to eat it for you."

I was impressed. Emma had gotten quite good at sign language. Mom said as much one afternoon when we went to visit a speech therapist for me and Emma. I saw Dad lower the corner of the newspaper and give Em a defying stare. Em hid her face behind her pudgy hands and got tomato sauce all over her face. I grinned at Dad, who winked at me. Emma was peeking through her fingers and saw the wink, but Dad went back to his stern look. Emma squealed and ran behind the couch.

Most of the days went by where I didn't think too much of what was going on. I joined a volleyball team in school, much to the surprise of my classmates. I only lasted three games before I quit. Well, I was kicked off the team.

"Anger management sounds better for you." the guidance counselor signed to me. Mom was so angry with me that she refused to look at me in the eye. She even made a point to move her chair so it was slightly not facing me. She wanted to make a point that she was mad but wanted to make sure I read her lips and saw her anger on her face. Oh, Mom. How endearing. I tried my best to not grin at the childishness of it. The guidance counselor saw my mouth twitching and lower her glasses at me. I glared at him and crossed my arms.

"Will the other boy be okay?" Mom asked without signing. I caught her lips moving and knew that is what she would ask. The guidance counselor raised her hands to sign, but Mom shook her head. The guidance counselor looked at me for a second, and then shook her head at Mom. "We can't single Simon out of the conversation in front of him," she signed. I gave Mom a defiant look. She shot me one of weariness.

That night, Dad grounded me for whacking the volleyball against another student. He asked me why I did it, and I signed that he never gave me the chance to get the ball myself. Dad tilted his head to one side, his way of telling me that he had no idea what I was talking about. He knew exactly what I was talking about but pretended that he had no idea what I was talking about. He tends to do this when he is trying to pretend he doesn't know, so I have to explain myself more. I hate it when he does this. Frustrated, I let out a cry of anger and hurriedly ran into the kitchen and got out the huge dry erase board on wheels. The first marker didn't work, and in anger, I threw it across the room. It hit Emma smack on the head. Emma looked up, startled, and then laughed.

Dad was livid. He marched over to me and grabbed my shoulder, squeezing as he grabbed. I refused to cringe. He was so angry he couldn't speak. We stared defiantly at each other, my chest heaving,

Dad's chest heaving. Dad's chest was heaving faster than mine. I moved my eyes from his glare and fixated my eyes to his chest. I tried to match our breathing. In and out. In and out. A few seconds later, we were in sync. Dad's breathing was calmer. Emma stared at us with interest, her big green eyes bulging out. Mom had snuck into the kitchen during this and was staring at us too. Never had they seen Dad grab me so roughly. I glanced at my shoulder slightly. Dad released me.

"I want to go up to my room," I signed.

Dad nodded. I went over to Emma, avoiding all eye contact with Mom, kissed Emma on the head where the marker hit her, and put the marker back on the dry erase board. Obviously it was silent for me, but Mom and Dad weren't saying anything. Emma grinned at me before I left the room.

Lying on my bed upstairs, stomach facing down, I pulled out a ratty old notebook. The Toronto Raptors logo was embossed on the cover. I had stuck a "Mean People Suck" sticker right over the raptor. What was I planning on writing on that dry erase board? I rolled over and searched under my bed for a pen or anything to write with. None. Sighing, I heaved myself up from my bed and grabbed a pen from my knapsack. Jumping back on my bed, I made myself comfortable. I wiped the beads of sweat off my forehead. I held a palm to my cheek and realized it was warm. I opened the notebook and saw scribbles of a poem I was trying to write to Nathalie. I ripped them out and crumpled them. Aiming, I threw them into the garbage can across the room. I missed. Story of my life.

My pen hovered over a fresh new page. What was I going to write? What was I going to write on that dry erase board? Pursing my lips, I took a deep breath. I took another one. One more. I took one last deep breath and tried to imagine that I filled my lungs.

Then I began to write.

Chapter 4

Dad and Mom never brought up the incident. I sure has hell didn't. My notebook knew though. My notebook knew how I felt. I didn't sleep at all that entire night. I had somehow discovered the joy of writing down my feelings. It was different; my whole life, I have been writing in order to communicate to my parents, to Emma, to my social workers, to my teachers, to my friends, to the post office. But never had I ever written for myself. Never had I ever let myself go. I didn't know what to say, what to write. I never formulated a full sentence before that didn't require some sort of direction, some sort of feeling that I was angry, that I was upset and how I felt inside.

"Dad made me angry. I was so angry. Not at Dad. But I was angry. I don't know why I'm angry," I signed to my social worker, Darah, the following day that I started writing in a journal. We had gone to a McDonald's for french fries and coffee, and I was on my fourth fry. Darah was on her second cup of coffee. I liked the word "journal" better than a "diary." She was surprised. "A journal?" she signed back. Her one brow raised up in the air. I followed suit. She saw my expression and laughed. "You can't do it," she signed, smiling. I didn't quite catch her sign. I shook my head and she wrote down on what she calls her "Simon pad." I read it upside down and tried again. I raised my eyebrow up again. She tilted her head to one side and watched me. With her finger, she pointed up. I tried harder. Laughing, she shook her head. Waving her hand, she signed, "A journal?"

Back to business. I nodded eagerly and signed, "I just started writing in a journal last night. I didn't sleep because I didn't realize that I had so much to say," I signed. Darah sat back, and took a sip of her coffee thoughtfully. I grabbed the pen and wrote down on the Simon pad. "Did

I do something wrong?" Darah looked down on what I wrote and shook her head fiercely.

"Simon, of course you didn't. I just wish I had known that maybe you had something inside that you wanted to express," she wrote down. I glanced at her.

"Of course I do. You're a social worker, isn't that your job to know this?" I asked.

Even Darah couldn't be taken aback from what I wrote. She was used to my bluntness. In fact, she said she "encouraged" it. A few weeks ago, I had said some hurtful things to her, without realizing that they were hurtful. I told her that she had gained too much weight, and she looked surprised at me. It was only because I saw her ripping eight packets of white sugar into her coffee. Well, she only got seven packets, but I handed her another one to make the number even.

"Yes, it is my job Simon, but I don't know everything," Darah signed. "Everything is a learning process. Every day I learn something new. From you or my other clients," she signed. I nodded.

"I am glad that you started to write. Do you feel comfortable in showing me what you wrote?" she signed. She wants to read what I wrote? Darah saw my expression. "You don't have to. I'm just asking," she signed. I grabbed the pad. "It's private," I wrote. Darah nodded.

"Of course, Simon. You are entitled to what you write. Well, there is an exercise I need you to do for me."

I cocked my head to one side. "What?" I signed.

"You are going to write in that book every single night, and every time you have the urge to write."

I rolled my eyes. "I was already planning on doing that," I signed.

"Good. That's all I ask."

I looked at her. "You're not going to ask me to show it to you, will you?" I signed. Darah shook her head. "You're not going to ask me to show it to my parents, will you?" I signed. Darah shook her head again. Hm . . . there had to be a catch. This seemed too easy. I can already picture my innermost thoughts and desires in Mom's hands and her embarrassment in what I wrote.

Darah shook her head again. She wrote on the Simon pad. "Simon, this is just between you and me. Everyone needs to release their thoughts and fears, and it never occurred to me to tell you to write it down." Darah blushed. "It's my own fault for assuming that you would be into sports instead. That was very closed-minded thinking on my part."

I agreed. Darah saw me nod and laughed. "Well, I hate to be your notebook, Simon. If you're this blunt and honest with me, I can't even think of what your notebook tolerates from you."

Every day after school, I went to a coffee shop and sat down to write. I found that coffee shops seemed relaxing. Everyone else seemed to be writing too, or doing schoolwork. I picked a seat in the back corner and with a pen, I started to write. Mostly about my day, but I found that it is easier to write about my feelings as time went on. At night, I started to pick up reading again. I was not a huge fan of reading, but I started to read again.

At night, I had started in on the Harry Potter series. I was going through *Harry Potter and the Philosopher's Stone*, which was a copy of Emma's that Mom was reading Emma to. I always was a bit envious of the fact that Mom would read to Emma, as I would have loved that kind of special ritual they had every night. But Mom still had a slight accent, and I felt it was kind of weird to watch Mom's lips. Especially at my age. I wrote about this in my journal. I also started reading books written by John Grisham. I wanted to read Stephen King but Dad had noticed what section I was on one evening when we both made a trip to the bookstore. Dad looked at me and steered me clear out of the horror section.

"No, Simon," he signed. I didn't argue. I had been staring at *Cujo* and decided that dogs were friendly pets, even if the cover of *Cujo* said no. *Cujo* reminded me of werewolves. I do not like werewolves.

"Read some other things first. If you really want to read horror, we'll ease into it," Dad signed. Good idea.

Reading helped me write. What I was thinking in my head was different from what I was really feeling. How I would sign was different from how I would write. I noticed that right away. I couldn't express myself as freely as I would like, because there are words that I don't know how to use in a sentence. Dad signed to me once that he's never seen me go to the bathroom so much. Mom was concerned.

"I read better when I'm in the toilet," I signed. Dad let out a laugh. Mom gave me a weary smile. The next afternoon, Dad, Mom, and Emma went to Ikea and bought a bookcase for the bathroom. I was left to read and write alone. "in peace," as Mom claims. I thought that was funny and signed so. Mom shrugged. "Just because you can't hear us doesn't mean that our presence can be bothersome." Mom sign-spelled "bothersome." She made a mistake with the "s" and I corrected her. Emma laughed and copied. Grinning, I grabbed her around the waist and gave her a big hug.

She hugged back, her chubby fingers circling my neck. I sniffed her hair, drew back, and signed to her. "You smell like strawberries."

Emma tilted her head to one side and signed, "I don't understand." It was the one sign phrase she and Dad perfected. I repeated the phrase; this time, I sign-spelled "strawberries." Emma grinned and took a strand of her hair, making a big show of taking a deep sniff. I laughed.

They came back later in the evening after I completed a John Grisham novel. I was instantly a fan. I was in the middle of writing how great the book was in my journal when my family came home. I watched from the staircase as Mom held the front of the box while Dad guided from the back. I laughed and signed, "Just like your marriage!" Mom gave me a look and Dad winked. Emma laughed. Mom turned around and looked at her, signing as she spoke. "What is so funny, Em?" Emma made a face and ran out of the room. I laughed. I went to help them open the box, but I ended up counting the boards and the nails instead. Slowly. Annoyed, Dad asked me to go back to my room and read another book. I didn't leave until I finished counting the rest of the nails in the little plastic bag it came in.

"For godssakes . . . ," Dad muttered. I caught his lips from the corner of my eye and ignored him. "Simon, there are about fifty nails in that bag," Dad signed. I nodded and signed back. "Yes. Forty-five more to go." Mom put a hand on Dad's arm and motioned him to come into the kitchen with her. Just as I finished counting the last of the nails, Dad came out, holding a steaming cup. I inhaled and made a face. "Tea?" I signed. Dad ignored the question. "Are you done, son?" he asked with one hand. I grinned and held up the bag. Dad smiled wearily and grimaced as he took a sip of his steaming cup of tea. Setting it down, he signed, "You should be able to count them again. I have to wait until this tea cools down."

The bookcase was big enough to fit into the bathroom. It was right in front of the toilet. In fact, one didn't even have to move from their spot on the toilet seat in order to get a book, unless you wanted to read a book from one of the higher shelves. Happily, I hurried to put my books in the bookcase in the bathroom. Emma tagged along, carrying a few more books. I was disappointed to see that all my books could fit into only half a shelf. There were eight shelves all together.

"Don't worry, Simon, we can always get more books," Mom signed when I stated this during dinner the next evening. Dad looked up from his chicken soup. "We have some books that we can put in the bathroom," he said.

Even when I wasn't in the toilet, I sat in that bathroom, on the toilet bowl, with the seat pulled down. One night, I fell asleep on the linoleum floor, in the middle of the fourth Harry Potter book. I had started on the toilet, but somehow toppled off and onto the floor. I woke up the next morning with a blanket on top of me and Emma's favorite Care Bear beside me. I thought that was funny and hugged Emma to tell her so the next morning.

Only Emma shares that bathroom with me during the night. Mom and Dad have their own bathroom in their bedroom. If I was not reading on the toilet, I was in the coffee shop writing. Mom asked one evening what I was writing. I shrugged her off.

"Is it private?" she asked. I nodded. "Very," I signed.

Mom smiled. "Will you let me read what you write?"

I shook my head with vehemence. "No, Mom!" I signed.

Mom laughed and grabbed me around the shoulders. "I would never invade your privacy, Simon," Mom signed. I gave her a skeptical look. I didn't believe her. She could tell. She "crossed" her heart with one finger. I still gave her a skeptical look, but I believed her now. She wouldn't do that unless she meant it. I took the book with me to dinner. Mom and Dad didn't mind. I think they were relieved that they didn't have to sign while eating.

One time, Dad was signing to me about how angry he was at the mailman for something, and he held his fork while he was signing. Accidentally, it flew out of his hand, complete with a piece of meat through it, and hit our white curtain. Mom was livid. It is easy to forget though, to put everything down, while signing to me during dinner. Even having me as part of the family for years, it is easy to forget. One time, Dad was cutting roast beef with a sharp knife and Dad tried to sign something to me. Mom's eyes bugged out and she ran to Dad and took the knife from him.

Dad is the worst when it comes to signing. He gets so passionate with telling me something as simple as "It's over there" and will let go of anything in his hands. So I didn't blame her. It was a very sharp knife. I should know, I was with Mom the day we ordered it through an infomercial.

I got quite good at writing. It was easy to write, even though how I was thinking in my head was a lot different than what I was saying. Within a few weeks, I had filled out two journals. Dad bought me a filing cabinet for my room with lock and key so that I can keep my journals locked up. I was really touched by this. I smiled at him. Dad shrugged it off, embarrassed. "It was in a garage sale when I was walking by," Dad signed. "No big deal." It was a big deal. I wanted a lock for my room too. I didn't know how to ask for one. Not that Emma, Mom and Dad would ever come into my room, but I wanted the possibility of locking it. I didn't want to ask yet though. I wanted to wait.

The bathroom had a lock and I was very comfortable being in there. The reason why I enjoyed being in the bathroom a lot too was because I started writing . . . well, short stories of my own. In one of the novels I was reading, I had picked up a book at a drugstore. The book was pricey for me, but I still wanted it. I would probably have needed some coins to pay for it, but I never carried coins with me. They always came in odd numbers, and the dimes are too small. The book had a man and woman staring passionately into each other's eyes. On the cover, she was wearing a dress with her shoulders showing. Her hair was flowing in the wind in the picture. I couldn't see the wind, but her hair was flying west. The man had long blond hair, his white shirt buttons were down (sort of like the one Dad uses for work, but never with that many buttons down), and there was a sunset in the background.

So of course, I bought it one day after school when I was alone. It took me three weeks of going to the drugstore every day to build the courage to buy the book. One of the cashiers who worked there saw me every day, and at first he looked at me suspiciously. I kept him in full view at all times. One day though, I felt a tap on my shoulder. I jumped. It was the cashier. He said something, and I shook my head and tried to sign. He looked taken aback and then I pointed to his lips, my face turning red. He understood quickly. Slowly, he said, "Is there anything I can help you with?"

I read his lips and didn't know how to sign "Yes, I want to buy that book that has the incredibly hot woman and somewhat undeserving man looking into each other's eyes so deeply. I want to know why that book is so thick, and what it could possibly be about. Please don't think I'm weird." Feeling my face get red deeper, I shook my head and quickly jotted down in a mininotepad from my pocket. "No, thanks, I'm just looking." He nodded, following his gaze to where I was standing. The entire rack was full of books of the woman with the bare shoulders and the man in the buttoned-down shirt. There was a particular one with them already in a bed. I wanted that one.

The cashier's eyes smiled kindly, although his lips didn't show it. He picked up the book that I was looking at and motioned me with his head to follow him to the counter. The store was empty. Thank goodness. I followed him to the front and he scanned the book for me, punched in a few numbers and pointed to the price: $8.97. Maybe I read the price wrong before. My budget was $ten.00. I quickly pulled out a ten-dollar bill and handed it to him, staring intently at the floor. He didn't flinch. I looked up and tried to catch his name on his name tag: "Tyler." (Thank you Tyler.) He handed me the receipt tucked inside the book and went on to help the customer who had inadvertently crept up behind me.

I took the book quickly and, without looking, at him, I half-jogged out of the store. Once I was out of view, I looked down at the book and pulled out the receipt to toss in the garbage. I always toss out receipts. I don't like them. I noticed though, that there was writing on the back of the receipt as I crumbled it. I rolled it back out.

"This is one of my favorites. Look for me when you're done with this one and I'll recommend some more."

Turning it over, I saw, that he had put his employee discount in, which is why I could afford the book in the first place.

It was my first taste of erotica. I devoured it. I ate it up with a spoon. I always knew that my eyes were more enhanced because I relied on them so much to get through life, but the words that dripped on the book, the imagery that was presented to me . . . I was in heaven. I have never read something that brought such vivid pictures in my mind. It took me awhile to actually open the book, I savored the cover alone for a few nights. I was scared to open it. I knew what it was about. Yet I didn't know what it was about. I wanted to know what it was about. I was scared to know what it was about. I knew nothing at all about what it was about. I was so scared to read it.

Holding the book alone stirred something inside of me that I didn't know much about. It also stirred a lot down there, um, between the legs as well. I don't know if "stirred" is the correct word. If it was "stirred" I could still stand up. There were nights when I simply couldn't stand up just because . . . well. You know. It was too exciting to read. And I mean that literally. Just touching the cover of the book gave me an erection. To make myself, um, settle down, I wrote in my book about how much I loved my sister, Emma. Usually, just writing her name was enough for uhm, you know what, to play dead. I watched it once, it was like a flag going down half-mast. Inch by inch.

Emma. (One inch.) Emma is the best sister in the world. (Another inch.) Emma has the prettiest little sister green eyes in the universe. (Another inch.) Emma's feet smell like rotten eggs. (Dead.)

I was usually pretty sad when I was, uh, dead down there. It was a whole new discovery. I know that sounds stupid, as I had read once that baby boys get erections as soon as they are born, but to actually understand that this was truly not instinctive but was more like something you can enjoy, and now I was appreciating the feelings of it.

Don't get me wrong, I was embarrassed too. A little overwhelmed. I felt like I stepped into a whole new world and everyone else I knew was in that world as well, but had their own versions of it. Every chance I got, I fantasized.

Rapt, rapt, rapt. I looked up. Dad had this stern look on his face. He was banging the end of his spoon on the table. "Simon?" he signed. I smiled, my face reddening. I felt like Dad knew exactly what I was thinking about. I felt like I was easily read, open like a Dr. Seuss book. Emma caught my expression and giggled. Mom, smiling slightly, looked at me while she passed a bowl of pasta over to me. With her hands free and mine full, she signed. "Who is she?" Emma laughed. I turned even redder and slammed the bowl of pasta on the table. I shook my head and finger spelled slowly. "No one." Mom looked like she was willing to amuse me a little more. She nodded and glanced at Dad. Dad was suddenly very focused on getting the spaghetti to stay on his fork. It was too much. Was all started to laugh.

Chapter 5

Dad knew of a friend who had a friend who had a friend who had a friend who had an opening at his butcher shop. I wanted a part-time job. Mom was a bit skeptical, but after Dad explained that working some odd hours a few times a week would give me some freedom and responsibility, Mom obliged.

"I supposed your father is right," Mom signed the night before I was to start working at the butcher shop. She sign-spelled "supposed" wrong. I didn't correct her. We were arranging the dining room table for a Scrabble game. Dad had bought a new board, the sleek kind with the raised letters on the board so that the letters don't move. It was a present for my first part-time job.

I was putting away Emma's *Highlights* magazines and storing them in a bookcase in the other room. As I was piling them up on the bottom-shelf, I noticed one of my books in the shelves! I recognized the colored spine. My eyes bulged out. I quickly pulled it out of the shelf and tucked it into the front pocket of my hooded sweater. "Kangaroo pocket," as Emma liked to call them. Emma and I had quite a few sweaters with kangaroo pockets. Most of our sweaters matched. I think that is one thing I will never outgrow with my sister.

I turned to Mom quickly as soon as I felt my breathing was calmer and signed, "I'll be right back. Washroom." And quickly ran upstairs before Mom could sign to me that I didn't have to run upstairs to use the washroom when there was one just next to the bookcase. Part of me wanted to laugh hysterically, part of me felt as red as a tomato. If Mom didn't see me come down in five minutes, she would come upstairs and into my room. I took a deep breath, but my face got even warmer. Where did I leave the book? In the washroom? Lying around in my room? No,

I'm good with hiding my books! Or have I been careless? How long as this one been downstairs?

I shut my door quickly and pulled the book out of my pocket. I remembered the spine, but not the cover. Not the cover . . . huh? What kind of cover was this? Wait, I don't remember buying this one . . . same woman. Same man. Different position. Much less clothing. Oh shit. This isn't mine. Same series. Not my book. This isn't my book. This isn't my book! This isn't my book? Ew! Whose book is it then? Mom's? Dad's? Obviously not Emma's, right?

I shoved the book at the bottom of my knapsack. Mom never goes in there. I had spilled a bottle of ginger ale once and forgotten about it, and Mom hated the smell of ginger ale. My knapsack was made of cloth too, so the smell stayed. She never came close to it and offered to buy me a new one every time she saw it. I kept saying I still wanted it. I looked out into the hallway and saw that Dad was getting ready to flick the lights on and off to tell me to hurry up. I ran out of the hallway and Dad look startled.

"Hurry, Si. Let's play," he signed as he held up the Scrabble dictionary. I followed him downstairs, trying to not think about whose book it belonged to. That night, I lost my very first Scrabble game. I refused to look at my parents. Let's just say my head wasn't in it. I was already thinking up new ways to buy a safe for my room.

I started my new job the following day. My job was what my dad liked to call "under the table," meaning that I was working without any strings attached. I was looking forward to it. I would work every Saturday from 2:00–6:00 p.m., and after school on Fridays from six to ten. Dad took me to work with a couple of pads of paper, a box of new pens and a small portable dry erase board. I met my boss, Jeff, who had written his name in *huge* letters on a name tag, also on the front of his apron and across his white hat. A friendly man, who said he owned his butcher shop, which he inherited from an uncle whom he grew up with. He had written out a huge description of himself, which he handed to me the moment we shook hands. He had written everything in point form:

> *My name is Jeff I'm 61 years old. I'm a Cancer. I'm married and have 3 daughters. My wife and daughters are all vegetarian, so my career upsets them. Flick the lights if you need me*
>
> *Don't ever worry about wanting to get my attention I listen to Franki Valli and the Four Seasons all the time. (But*

he ended up crossing it out, probably realizing that it meant nothing to me.)

Call me anytime. My assistant, Nick, can speak your language and said he can help you anytime. Don't be shy. But please tell us when you are not comfortable with doing anything. Please try to talk in your language to me. I want to learn how to sign.

I grinned and looked up at Jeff, who seemed exceedingly proud of his list. He also gave a copy to Dad. Jeff looked so excited, like he was ready to jump out of his apron. He jumped up and put a finger in the air and ran behind the counter to where there was a small room. Five seconds later, he wheeled out a huge dry erase board that had a crooked ribbon stuck on the top. He had written across it "WELCOME SIMON" and, before he could do a little dance, he presented a package of new dry erase markers with a flourish. Even Dad had to laugh.

Jeff jumped across the board with a grand sweep of his arm, then tapped Dad and said, "Does he like it?" Since he spoke slowly, I could read his lips. Dad was going to translate and saw that I already understood. I nodded with a huge smile and pulled out a marker. On the board I wrote "Thank you so much."

Jeff showed me and Dad around the butcher shop, explaining what he could, and having Dad translate it for me. I was basically going to start off by cleaning the shop. Jeff explained to Dad that there were a lot of things that would be taught as time went on, but to ease me into it, I had to familiarize myself with the shop first. I didn't mind.

Jeff also explained that Nick would be teaching me how to make the meat, how to make sausages, how to package the meat, etc. And that will take some time and observing. Nick would be coming in next week; he had taken a week off to study for exams. Jeff explained to Dad that Nick was a student who came from a huge family and was the only one out of his four brothers and sisters who was not deaf. He could hear perfectly well and speak clearly, but was the only one of his entire family who could. Both his parents were also deaf.

As the youngest in his family, he was the only one who was born with perfect hearing. He was a student at a nearby university studying Social Work and Political Science, and was saving up to volunteer in a country I never even heard of. Nick was just five years older than me too, but had such huge goals. I couldn't wait to meet him.

"How was your first day on the job, Simon?" Emma signed to me when I came home. Mom came out of the kitchen and I kissed her on the cheek. I laughed and signed, "As good as could be expected." She tilted her head to one side, and Mom hit me with a dishrag. "Use words your sister can understand, Sai," I sign-spelled. *"amazing"* and Emma squealed. She wrote on her dry erase board. "What did you do? Did you kill a cow?"

Now it was Emma's turn to get hit by a dishrag. With Mom's back slightly facing away from me, I couldn't read her lips clearly, but I could see her telling Emma that I didn't work in a farm and that I wasn't doing anything drastic. Then I saw Mom's back stiffen. She turned and looked at me. "You're not actually killing animals, are you?" she signed. Dad laughed as he caught the end of the question. Dad winked at me. "Your son here killed four cows today!" Emma's eyes bugged out.

"Four!" she mouthed silently. She slinked behind the table, looking at me like I was going to butcher her next. I played along. I nodded dramatically and held up four fingers. Mom started playing along too until she saw that Emma's eyes started to tear up.

"Okay, okay. Enough," Mom said. Dad laughed and tried to grab Emma. Emma dodged Dad's huge hands and darted out of the room. Mom looked at Dad and me with exasperation. I laughed.

Dad put an arm around my shoulder and squeezed. "Your son here did no such thing. He cleaned." I couldn't see Dad, and he wasn't signing, just explaining to Mom. I knew, though, when to grin.

"You better go and talk to your sister," Mom said, trying to stay mad, but I could see the smile playing around her lips. I grinned back and nodded. "Yes, ma'am," and went to Emma's room. Emma wasn't in her room, though. I checked the washroom. She wasn't there, either. I had a sudden jolt in my stomach. I went into the end of the hall to my room. There she was. Emma was sitting on my bed. Reading the exact book I had pulled off the shelf. She looked up, out of fear, but for some reason, I sensed it was because she thought I had butchered four cows, not that I had caught her reading a very inappropriate book for a nine-year-old.

For some reason though, I wasn't mad. I was doing exactly the same thing. I was a little more surprised at how calm Emma was. I felt guilty, at the age of seventeen, for reading these books, where Emma was nine years old, and she clearly didn't think she had done anything wrong. Or maybe she just hasn't gotten caught yet.

"Where'd you get that book?" I signed, sitting next to her. I didn't bother to close the door. Mom and Dad never disturb me when I'm having a sister moment. They think it's really "cute."

"You left it in your bag." Emma smiled. She dog-eared a page and sat up. Signing, she asked, "Did the cows cry?" Huh? Oh yeah. I killed four cows at work today.

"Dad was just joking. Can you please tell me why you are reading this book?" I asked. I felt a little wild. Does she even know what the books mean? What they are talking about?

"I found a copy at the library, and it didn't have a bar code. I bought it for ten cents," Emma explained. "Did you like it?"

I felt my face turn red. How do you answer such a question to a nine-year-old? She asked me as calmly as if she was asking me how the weather was. I all of a sudden felt younger than my nine-year-old sister.

"I haven't read it yet," I signed carefully. "How did you like it?" Geez, am I actually having this conversation? I shook my head wildly. "Emma, do you even know what these books are about?" I signed. I made my eyes as big as pancakes. Well, the pancakes Mom makes. Dad's are too tiny.

"Yes." Emma nodded seriously. "It's about sex." She sign-spelled "sex." I looked at her with disbelief.

"Do you even know what sex is?" I signed back. Emma's face didn't change. I still couldn't believe I was having this conversation with my sister.

"Of course, Sai! Everyone knows what sex is!" I felt very small, all of a sudden. Of course, I knew that.

"Emma, are you not too young to be reading this?" I signed. There. That is exactly what I was trying to get out.

"No. I'm nine years old." Good point.

But . . ."Emma, it's erotica."

"What's erotica?"

Shit. Even I didn't know. There was a question I wanted to ask so badly. Should I dare?

"Emma, when you read the book, do you do anything to your body?" Emma raised an eyebrow. "Like what?"

"Things, Emma. *Things*." I was starting to get annoyed. Was I really having this conversation?

Emma cocked her head to one side. She was getting annoyed too. "What do you mean by 'things'? Turning the page with my fingers?"

I jumped off the bed and stomped both feet on the ground. I was getting so angry. Emma jumped off my bed too and stomped with me. I never had to stomp on the ground with her, only with our parents, and she always joined me when I did. I kept stomping until I had a rhythm. Emma's feet started to stomp along with me. I got even more annoyed. I screamed. Emma's eyes jumped out, and she ran out of my room.

I ran to my door and shut it. I leaned my back against the door and let myself slide down. I didn't know how I was feeling, but I was annoyed. Why do I feel so guilty about reading these books? Why was Emma okay with reading them? Was it appropriate to ask her what she did with her body? Am I allowed, as her brother, to ask such a question? Would she go and tell Mom and Dad? Now, they will know what I read. Will they make fun of me? Will they have a talk with me?

I felt like my space, that part of my mind where I liked to fantasize, was violated. It was a guilty pleasure of mine, to go into that place in my mind and let myself go. Now, I felt like a joke because Emma obviously didn't seem to even flinch at the idea of reading erotica books, whereas I was trying so hard to hide them. Am I wrong? Was it okay to be open about them? Why I was I feeling so guilty?

I felt something poke me in the bum. I skidded forward and turned around. Emma's fingers were protruding under the door. I stood up and fiddled with the knob. She wiggled her fingers. Peace. She wanted peace. Or the book, I don't know. I was afraid to open the door, what if she called Mom and Dad and told them that we both read the same kind of books? Clearly inappropriate? I took a deep breath and ran my hand through my hair. Then I opened the door a bit. Emma was lying on the floor on her stomach. She jumped up when she saw me. She stuck out her bottom lip. "Don't be mad at me, Si" she signed. I wasn't mad at her. I opened my arms and she ran into them. It was then that I realized, I needed someone to talk to. Trying to figure things out for myself was not going to help me.

"Emma, did you tell Mom and Dad that you read these books?" I signed. Emma shook her head. Hmm. "Why not?" I asked. Emma leaned forward and looked over her shoulder. Then, appearing to whisper, she signed, "I don't think I'm supposed to read them."

I signed inwardly. Thank goodness. I'm not crazy. "Why not?" I asked, as calmly as I could. "Mommy reads them too, but she always tries to hide them when I come into the room." Emma pointed to the book which was lying on my bed. "That one is Mommy's."

I guess my prayers were answered. I met Nick the following week and I was in awe. Everything about Nick was everything I wish I was. He was confident, handsome and very, very kind. He carried a picture of his girlfriend in his wallet, a beautiful woman named Rachel, whom he had met on a trip to Morocco.

"I'm from Morocco!" I signed to him when he first told me. Nick had volunteered in Morocco a few years back in an orphanage in Rabat. I explained that I was adopted by my parents in an orphanage in Rabat. Unfortunately, it wasn't the same one, but we still marveled at the coincidences. Nick spoke as fluently in ASL as I did, as those who were taught properly spoke. He always signed when he was around me, and also spoke in English too while signing.

All of a sudden, I had a confidant. Nick was easy to speak to. I felt such a rapport with him the second I was introduced to him. I found that communicating with the large dry erase marker was mostly for Jeff, who was in awe of how Nick and I communicated with each other. I watched too, just how loved Jeff was, as I was able to observe how Jeff spoke to his many customers. He always introduced me and instructed those he introduced me to to wave.

He had common customers who bought meat every Friday and every Saturday. One man bought the same six pounds of ground chicken every Friday. His name was Jedd. A tall Asian man, whose head was peppered with white hair. He wore glasses that didn't seem to fit and always wore the same jean jacket. Even when it was too cold to wear one. He was very friendly, though, and always waved when he saw me, and seemed to be a good friend of Jeff's. I signed to Nick once. "What does he do with all that meat?"

Nick signed back. "His family loves spaghetti and he has two children ages fourteen and twelve. He works evenings most of the week, so he cooks spaghetti and leaves it in the fridge. The kids eat the spaghetti on the nights he comes home late from work."

"What about their mom? Does she not cook?" I signed.

Nick shook his head. "She left them years ago. Jedd has been coming here for years, since his kids were babies, and never misses a Friday night. Jeff always gives a little more than he asks and charges less. He's got a soft spot in his heart for Jedd. His wife left him without so much as a note."

After working for a month, I received two checks already and was pretty happy with receiving the cash. I also had grown very close to my coworkers, who were Nick, Jeff, and another man who comes in during the week except Saturday, and Rudy, a Peruvian man, who was just as jolly and friendly as Nick. He was not fazed at all by my inability to hear, and actually saw that it was fun to write out notes and write on the dry erase board. I only saw him for an hour only, as he left on Friday as soon as I came in.

One Friday evening, Jeff wrote on the dry erase board to me. "Would your parents allow you to come to a karaoke bar with us tonight?" Nick was standing nearby with a grin on his face. He was ready to translate at any given moment. I shrugged. Friday nights were Scrabble nights, but we had moved it to Saturday nights, with the occasional Sunday nights when I started working. Mom was a bit overprotective of me working so late into the night on Friday nights that she picked me up every shift with Emma in tow. Her excuse was buying meat when she picked me up, and bought a week's worth of supply every Friday.

"If it is for next Friday, I am sure I can ask," I signed. "My mom would get upset if it was tonight. I didn't give her notice." Nick translated it for me.

"That's perfect!" Nick was translating for me. "We can go next Friday! It isn't opened yet anyways this week."

"Is it new?" I signed.

"Very." Jeff grinned. "It's my own. Well, my wife and I are opening it." I guess, when you're deaf, you don't know much about office gossip unless it's signed to you.

"You are opening your own bar?" I signed back. Wow. I looked around the butcher shop, which is at least the size of our kitchen at home.

"Karaoke bar," Nick sign-spelled.

"What's that?" I signed. Nick's eyes almost fell out of its socket, but he quickly recovered. He nodded understandingly.

"Ask your parents to come next week," he signed with a smile. "Or even better, ask them to come." I know I'm seventeen years old, but the fact Nick had signed to invite my parents made me feel a little better. One, it is now socially acceptable since they were invited by Nick. Two, well, to me, a bar is a bar. I have never been to a bar.

"Would my nine-year-old sister be allowed?" I signed. Jeff nodded eagerly. He reminded me of one of the bobbleheads Dad had on his dashboard.

"Yes, your nine-year-old sister can come," he wrote on the dry erase.

When I got home I asked my parents to explain what a karaoke bar was. Both were extremely excited to go.

"A singing bar," Dad signed. I looked at them. "Singing?" Even Emma nodded with them in unison.

"How can I go to a bar that sings?" I signed.

"We can sing ourselves. The words are on a machine. And everyone kind of sings along." Dad wrote this on the dry erase board in the kitchen. I gave them a look.

"I'm deaf," I signed.

Mom gave me a mock look of surprise. "You are?"

Dad grinned. "You can read the words off the machine thing. I don't know if we can all read it, but it's a different atmosphere. Something new." I have never been to a karaoke bar before, and was curious so I was looking forward to going after work the following Friday. I was a little annoyed, though, that I wouldn't be able to hear anything, but I was looking forward to soaking everything else just by looking. I had no idea what to expect.

Just before my parents picked me up and we closed the shop on Friday, Jeff grinned at me. "I had things changed around when I met you, when you started working for me. I had the machine changed into a big screen so everyone can sing along," Jeff told Nick, who translated with a grin. When I had a chance to speak to Nick alone, I signed to him. "Did he really change things around so its more accommodated to me?" Nick nodded with a fond grin. "He really likes you. He thinks you're a good kid."

Jeff's karaoke bar was called Taking the Wheel. It used to be a diner/ fisherman's restaurant, and Jeff just played around with the atmosphere, since the inside of the bar looked like a ship. There was a massive huge screen on the front of the bar, and the lighting was very bright. Emma was jumping up and down with excitement. We ordered food, and Mom seemed relieved to see that there was a kids' menu as well.

As someone who is deaf, I cannot listen to music. I have always been curious as to listening to music, as I know my parents often play CDs. When I was younger, about six, my dad was listening to a tape cassette of Bob Marley and was sitting on the floor with earphones on. That struck me as hilarious because Mom was working that day, but Dad still had his earphones on. I signed this to Dad with a grin, I remember, and he laughed too when he realized that he didn't need the earphones. He took them off and had me sit on his lap and pulled out the lyrics from the cassette container. I had just started to read, and was thirsty to read more, so Dad started to lead me through the words as the song went on.

The first time I ever "read" a song was to "Three Little Birds." It was Dad's favorite song and we repeated this one several times. Dad's finger went along with the tune of the songs we sung together. I mouthed along with Dad with the words, since he often swayed with the music, or rocked back and forth. Another favorite of Dad's was the Beatles' "Imagine," in which he taught himself how to play on a little electrical keyboard that we bought once at a garage sale. I loved the lyrics to "Imagine." I often took the lyrics with me to bed, and would read the words just before I went to bed.

I had forgotten how much I enjoyed reading the words, even though I couldn't hear the tune. At the karaoke bar, I realized just how much I missed that short but rare time with my dad. I looked over at him and caught his eye, and he glanced at me and winked. I knew then, that he had remembered that special time we had when I was six years old. I had never seen my coworkers outside of work, so to see them very laid-back, more than usual, was unreal.

Jeff was first up. Nick leaned forward to us, his eyes dancing, and signed, "Jeff always sings to Frankie Valli and the Four Seasons. He always starts off with 'Sherry,' 'Walks Like a Man,' and then goes straight to 'Can't Take My Eyes Off You.'" Of course, none of this meant anything to me, but both my parents' faces told me that we were in for a good time.

Jeff went up to the stage excitedly. Already, there were people coming into the bar, and all of a sudden the words came unto the screen. I read along with the words, mouthed along, just the way I did when Dad and I were singing to Bob Marley and the Beatles. It was easier too, since the words would light up, indicating when you were supposed to sing along, pause, go faster or slower.

I didn't know who Frankie Valli and the Four Seasons were, but I was particularly fond of the words for "Can't Take My Eyes Off You." What wonderful words to sing to someone you care deeply about. When Jeff was done, Nick had gone up. I had seen him down a couple of beers, and he seemed a little more relaxed than usual. Nick's song selection was "Iris" by the Goo Goo Dolls, and "Stand by Me" by BB King. I had never read the words to these songs. It was fun, however, to see my parents and my sister, including Jeff and Rudy, sing along to the words of this song. I mouthed along with them.

My parents were too shy to go up, but Jeff coaxed my dad to finally go up after a few beers. Before going up, Dad finished the rest of his beer with Mom squealing with laughter next to him, whispered something to Jeff, who looked over at me and nodded, and then Dad was pulling me up on the stage with him. I laughed along with everyone, knowing that I couldn't make a complete fool of myself, since I would just stand up with Dad and watch him make a fool of himself. When we went up, the words to "Let It Be" came on. Dad made a face, and then signed to me saying. "I wanted 'Imagine,'" but I shook my head and smiled, signing. "It's fine." I didn't care. I wasn't as familiar with the words to this song, but I was familiar to the feelings of once again singing with my dad. I grinned out to the audience and saw my mom and sister beaming at me. I mouthed along with the words of the song, not hearing the tune, but feeling the music.

Chapter 6

Emma and I never spoke about the books of erotica, nor did I let her know that I was reading them. I had though, stopped buying them, as it was quite disturbing to know that I read the same erotica books as my nine-year-old sister and my forty-two-year-old mother. Although I had lost this sacredness fantasies I had, I did have a friend whom I confessed the books to. Nick looked like he was going to die from laughter when I signed the story of Emma reading Mom's erotica books. I was annoyed at first at how hard Nick was laughing, as this was clearly not a joke, but his laughter was contagious. His face had turned as red as a tomato, he was hugging his himself, laughing so hard, almost keeling over. I started laughing too. The following week, Nick handed me a large envelope, a smile dancing around his lips.

"What's this?" I signed. I tried to open the envelope, but Nick put a hand over mine and shook his head. "Private," he sign-spelled. I nodded.

That night, when I got home, after shutting the door, and making sure the entire house was asleep, I had my very first taste of porn. In magazine form.

Was I still feeling guilty? Not exactly. I had Nick to turn to, who seemed to have an endless supply of porn, and he knew exactly when I needed it. I started to sneak porn into school with me, as I finally decided to let the old knapsack go. The smell of ginger ale became too unbearable, especially when I left a tuna sandwich there for a few weeks in a secret pocket.

I didn't have many friends at school. There was one other person who was deaf in school, and although he was in a grade lower than me, we never really communicated with each other. You would think, two people, on the same boat, would have much to, um, say. His name was Adam. Adam Morrisey was his full name. We saw each other around in school, and always nodded with that half-smile, a sign of recognition that hey, I know you because we are both deaf, but we will probably never talk because we have nothing in common to talk about.

Aside from other students, I didn't really have any friends in school. I was never a subject of bullying, not the way they show it on television shows, but I was more like completely ignored. I never had to worry about pairing up for school projects because I was automatically put into independent studies. I also found that no one in school ever really reached out to me. No classmate ever tried to connect with me. I was fine with this, as I preferred to be alone. Most days, I kept to myself and wrote. I kept writing. I wrote endlessly, mostly about nothing, mostly about everything. Random words.

One day I found that I had written the word "banana" over and over again, before I realized that I was craving a banana. I signed this to my social worker when I had a chance. I was surprised that I had wasted three hours after school, sitting in the library, writing the word "banana" over and over again. I remembered how I had done this just a few weeks ago, I had written the word "breasts" over and over again. I thought it was because of the erotica books I was reading, so my face went beet-red, and I ripped the paper into shreds.

Bananas had nothing to do with erotica or the porn I was reading, so what did this have to do with anything? Without thinking, I admitted that I was quite into porn. My social worker Darah didn't even bat an eye. "Quite normal," she signed. I cocked my head to one side and just gave her a deadpan stare. She signed as she spoke. "You are exploring your sexuality. I would be very worried if you weren't."

"Okay, but what does this have to do with bananas?" I signed. Rachel tried to hide a smile. "I don't know. Maybe because they look like penises?" she signed, a serious look on her face. I looked down. Social worker or no social worker, I couldn't talk about this with her.

"I don't know where the last three hours went," I signed.

"Are things okay at home?" Rachel signed. I nodded.

"Work?" I nodded again. This time a little more vigorously. Work was fantastic. We went to Taking the Wheel every single Friday night.

"Maybe you just had a craving for a banana, Simon. There's no cause for alarm." She paused, and looked up. "Have you been writing in your journal?" I nodded. "Every day," I sign-spelled. Darah nodded thoughtfully. "Keep writing. Don't hold back."

Nick presented me one day with a DVD. He asked me if I had a DVD player or if I could watch DVDs on my computer. I signed that I was given a DVD player from one of my parents' friends a few months ago. It was a pretty extravagant gift, a gift that I felt like I didn't deserve since I was not close to this friend of my parents and it seemed like they were not very close to him either. But he insisted that I take it. As a birthday gift. His name was Makafui. I only met him that one time, as he lived in Ghana, and he was coming through Canada and the United States and decided to give my parents a call. He stayed with us for two nights, and on the second night, he gave me the portable DVD player and Emma a set of books, a series called *A Series of Unfortunate Events*. Emma's grin was as wide as the Cheshire Cat's.

Mom and Dad encouraged us to send a thank you card for this gift, and we did, as I had realized the freedom of having my own portable DVD player. We had one, a DVD player, downstairs in the family room, and we watched movies a few times a month as a family, but I was kind of outgrowing their movie choices.

Nick had given me a gem. He had given me my first DVD porn. Even though I always had the volume down to mute—because I found it saved the battery, and I obviously didn't need the sound—I kept checking the mute button when I watched my first porn. Okay, this was definitely much different than looking at pictures on a magazine. Much different. Double checking to see if my door was locked, I kept an eye at the door and gently rubbed my penis over my pants. It felt good. A relief, actually. I cringed. It felt too good. I felt my face turning warm, as I watched the bodies of an exceedingly handsome man and an even exceedingly beautiful woman mesh their bodies together in a way no picture in a magazine could.

With every strength I could muster, I pulled my hand away and shut the DVD. My heart was pounding, and I needed a glass of water. I sat up from my bed, and then realized that just because I had closed the DVD and pulled my hand away, it didn't mean that I was even close to be on the ground. I needed to go into the kitchen. I needed water. I knew that Dad had a tendency to just end up in the kitchen in front of the fridge.

Emma. (One inch.) Emma is the best sister in the world. (Another inch.) Emma has the prettiest little sister green eyes in the universe. (Another inch.) Emma's feet smell like rotten eggs. (Dead.)

There we go. I stood up, looked down to make sure I was safe, and then went downstairs to get a glass of water. No one else was in the kitchen. I filled a tall glass with ice-cold water, gulped it down, and then refilled it again. After the fourth cup of water, my heart stopped beating. I took a deep breath, and then felt my stomach rumble. Bathroom. I went upstairs and peed. Now, this handling of my penis, I was very familiar with. I peed for a whole five minutes. Dad had placed an alarm clock over the toilet seat when I started timing how long I urinated when I was five. We always had an alarm clock over the toilet seat since then.

Should I try again? I wanted to. I felt a shiver go up my spine at the mere thought of how it felt to touch myself. My thoughts quickly went back to the DVD. The DVD was apparently forty-five minutes long, and I had gotten turned on just by putting the DVD in. I was curious to know what else was in the DVD. All I had seen was three minutes of it, the introduction, and I was already . . . um, excited.

I thought back to what Darah had said. That this was normal. That exploring my sexuality was a normal thing and that she encourages it. I thought back to Nick, who seemed proud of his huge collection of porn, and who seemed very proud to be the one who was passing his treasures down to me. Washing my hands and leaving the bathroom, I casually glanced down at the hall. Emma's room was opened slightly, and my parents' room was completely shut and the lights were off. I half-jogged into my room and closed the door, locking it behind me. I opened the DVD player again, and suddenly felt goose bumps. I was filled with anticipation and excitement. I pressed the stop button, and then pressed play again. I was going to watch the entire DVD. No matter what.

I did. I didn't sleep that night. I kept watching and watching the same DVD, but I refused to touch myself, as much as I wanted to. I was extremely fascinated in the roles the actors were playing in the movie. The facial expressions, the close-ups, the positions, the teasing. I was fascinated by all of it. I was particularly fascinated with the facial expression of the woman in the movie. Although I couldn't hear her, I knew she was screaming with happiness. The first time I watched the entire DVD, I kept my eyes glued to the screen. I lay with my stomach flat and kept my hands as close to my face as possible. I rocked a bit here and there, but I refused to touch myself. I wanted to absorb everything, especially the woman's facial expressions. I kept my journal out and wrote down words that came to my mind about everything I was watching. I loved how her eyes were squeezed tightly, and her mouth was open as if she was experiencing the most wonderful feeling in the world. She looked angry, or was it frustrated? But wait, all of a sudden, she looked happy and was grinning, then she looked like she was in pain again. When it was done, the actual act of sex was only the last fifteen minutes of the DVD. The first half-hour was all acting.

"Foreplay," Nick explained the following Friday. For some reason, I felt very comfortable talking to Nick about this. He didn't laugh as much as he used to, and he seemed to enjoy the role of being the "big brother." I gave him a dumb look. Nick grinned and sign-spelled it. Then he tried to explain it by signing. I asked him to stop and to please use the dry erase. Nick obviously didn't know how to explain foreplay without using his entire body and I was afraid Jeff or Rudy would walk in. Nick laughed.

"Sorry, I'm the youngest in my family and no one has ever asked me before to explain what foreplay is," he laughed.

"Just write it as simple as you can," I signed.

Nick grabbed the marker and wrote, "The BEST part of sex is the anticipation of it." I looked at him, deadpan.

"That's all you need to know," he signed, with a wink. Nick handed me another DVD.

"This one is one of my favorites. It's yours to keep," he signed, grinning. I made a grab for it, and Nick pulled it away from me. "Make sure you hide these from your family," He signed. "I don't want to end up you telling me that your sister has watched all your stash and your parents watched it with her." I nodded adamantly, and he handed it to me. He smiled. "Welcome to reality," he signed.

That was one of the longest shifts at work I had. All I wanted to do was go home and watch the DVD. Of course, though, my parents had a Scrabble night planned. I wanted to say I wasn't interested in playing Scrabble that night, but I knew how important it was for us to play Scrabble together as a family. Besides, I wouldn't feel comfortable watching this DVD if my parents were still awake downstairs with Emma, playing Scrabble. Before I had said good night to Nick, who had driven me home, I admitted to him that I had yet to experiment with playing with myself.

"You have never masturbated yet?" Nick signed, slamming his foot on the brakes of his car.

I shook my head. Nick looked at me. "*Ever?*" he sign-spelled.

I shook my head. "Ever," I signed.

"In your entire life?" he signed.

I was getting mad, but Nick was having too much fun to notice. "Yes, in my entire life."

"How did you avoid that?" Nick asked, his face suddenly resuming brotherly concern. It was if, all of a sudden, it occurred to him that I may not be able to masturbate.

I noticed this immediately and signed, "I want to, and I can, I just haven't," I signed.

"But you are able to get erected," he signed.

I nodded. "All the time. It's embarrassing, actually," I signed back.

Nick looked relieved. "Do you want more porn?" he asked.

I gave him a look of exasperation. "Of course!" I signed.

"Then promise me that you'll masturbate tonight," he signed, his face as serious as a librarian. "I will not give you any until you actually masturbate to the point where you can't even touch yourself anymore."

We shook on it.

Well, of course, I wanted more. I loved porn. I was obsessed with porn. I wanted to watch as much as possible, every day if possible. And of course, I never break a promise. Well, I wasn't going to break this one. I just wish that Scrabble night would hurry up a little faster. My parents, however, had decided to extend the game as long as possible, for whatever reason unbeknownst to me. My head was hardly in the game, and unfortunately, my parents could read my face like a Dr. Seuss book. In fact, so could Emma.

"What is wrong, Simon?" Dad signed, when he finally tapped me on the shoulder. I had focused on staring at my Scrabble pieces: four Es, one T, one O, and A. I turned my tile over to show Dad. I didn't even have the motivation to play, but at least I can use my lack of good letters as an excuse. Dad cocked his head to one side, trying to see if he could make a word with my pieces. Emma wagged her finger at him, and Dad laughed. He handed me the bag and signed that I should change two of my Es. I did. I ended up pulling out a B and an S. Oh geez. I immediately turned red. Scooting over, so no one could read my tile, I arranged the letters B, R, E, A, S, T. I paused so long that Mom tried to look over. I glared at her and covered my tile.

"Simon, we don't have all night," Mom signed impatiently. I nodded, my face reddening even more. Do I dare? After all, it is a very innocent word. We had some for dinner tonight. In a mushroom-soup thing that made the whole kitchen smell like a forest. I looked at the words already made on the board. Perfect! There's an M, completely free. I joined the letters. "S, T, R, E, A" to the M and had the word "stream." I grinned. Safe.

Emma applauded and tallied up my points. I dove into the Scrabble bag again after giving it a good shake. I pulled out (I am not joking), S, C, U, M. I didn't even notice the S. Okay, I had to leave the room. I looked up and signed to my parents, "I don't feel too well. I think I should just go to bed." I didn't realize that Dad was looking at the letters I had pulled out from the corner of his eye. I saw him raise his fist to his mouth and clear his throat. His Adam's apple jumped up and down. He caught my eye, and I looked down quickly, throwing the four letters into the bag. I looked at Dad pleadingly. He must understand. He must have been a horny teen once too. He did. He did understand. He signed, while looking at Mom across the table. "He's got homework." (Boy, did I.)

I nodded seriously. "Lots," I sign-spelled. Mom look like she didn't believe either one of us, but that was okay. She obliged. Emma looked horrified that I was leaving the game before a winner was announced. I saw Mom trying to explain but didn't stick around to find out what she was signing to Emma about. I shot Dad a look of gratefulness, but he had a look on his face as though a lightbulb had just popped over his head. In my room, I shut and locked the door and even put my red beanbag in front of the door just in case. Should I? But they were still awake! If they wanted me, they would start flicking the light switch outside my room, which would make one of my lightbulbs flash on and off. I didn't want to risk it. I had a sinking feeling that my dad knew what was on my mind, and I needed to digest that first.

I wanted to fantasize about masturbating, fantasize about the woman in the first DVD, but I felt jumbled inside. I had all these things going on and I had no idea how to handle these thoughts. What I was thinking had nothing to do with what I was feeling. I wanted to think about what my dad was thinking of me now, but all I wanted to do was turn that DVD on. I knew that it was way early in the evening and my parents wouldn't be going to bed anytime soon. Emma was allowed to stay up late on Saturday as well, and she took full advantage of this. Part of me too, felt a bit bad, that I had walked away from the family ritual we have done for years. Was it okay to have walked away from that? I felt terrible deep down. I all of sudden felt a different kind of guilt. When did growing up become so complicated?

My lightbulb did not switch on at all that night. I didn't bother to write in my journal, nor did I put the DVD in. I instead put in a DVD of

The Adventures of Babysitting. Mom and I used to watch the movie with subtitles ever since it came out with subtitles, and one of my favorites. Mom had bought me the DVD as soon as it came out, since it was hard to read the words with the VHS. I loved Elizabeth Shue though, and so one evening, I came home from school back in the fifth grade to see that Mom had written out the entire script. I am not normally an emotionally ten-year-old boy, but that evening, I cried and held on to my darling mother as we watched the movie together. I knew how hard it was for her to write in English, and she had spelled some of the words wrong, but I still kept the script: I had tucked it into a huge book on bugs that was given to me as a gift one Christmas but was not too particularly fond of. The pictures of the spiders were too lifelike, but my sister was afraid of the book too, so I was able to hide papers such as these in the book without the fear of her taking it.

Now, they had DVDs with subtitles, but there were days when I would pull out Mom's script and read along with it. I could just imagine her sitting on the floor next to the VCR, because we had lost the remote control for the VCR, and writing down every single line by every single character in the movie. The beauty of the DVD player is there is no rewind button.

However, I longed to see a porn being played backward. At around midnight, I came out of my room, dressed as if I was ready for bed, when I knew that the night was still young. The lights were all off in the house. I turned on the hallway light, not embarrassed at all for being afraid of the dark at my age. When you don't have your hearing, your sight is everything. I went down to the kitchen, and as a decoy, got a glass of water. The kitchen was spotless. Mom had left the Scrabble game sitting on the table in the kitchen, but other than that, it was very clean. I went back upstairs, and opened Emma's door. A crown of her hair was scattered on her pillow. Good. At least she was asleep. I felt that my little sister could have a career as a ninja one day. She was extremely stealthy for her personality. Or maybe that was just because of me, not being able to hear her come. Regardless, she was a ninja. And her shadow seemed to terrify me sometimes, which struck me as weird, because she could hear me and we both would jump back. I would squeal to what I would imagine is an equivalent to a scream, but Emma was a full blown scream that always got my parents running from every direction of the house.

In the dead of the night, I pulled out the DVD that Nick had just recently given me. My body jumped with anticipation and all of a sudden, I felt goose bumps all over my body. I already felt a bit turned on just by turning on the DVD player. Taking a deep breath, I put the DVD in. I had promised Nick, hadn't I? I had to keep my promise to him no matter what. He made me spit on my hand too, which I refused, but then he wouldn't give me the DVD unless I did. Was this what guy friends did? I had no idea. But we shook hands after he spat in his hand as well, and I wiped my hand on the seat of his car before leaving it. I felt him hit me when I did.

I popped the DVD in, and waited a few seconds before the screen came on. Then I realized that I should go and wash my hands. I put the pause button on, and went to the bathroom. I realized then too that I had to pee, then washed my hands. I timed myself. ten minutes to wash my hands. I got more soap and washed it again for another ten minutes. After thirty minutes in the bathroom, I finally got my breathing intact. I was breathing deeply. In through my nose, out through my mouth. In through my nose, out through my mouth. In through my nose, out through my mouth. Okay. I'm ready. I turned to walk out of the bathroom and walked right into Dad.

I jumped back and signed frantically. "What are you doing up?" Dad rubbed his eyes from the sudden light in the bathroom. He was the only one who went to the bathroom in the dark, because he always got in trouble with Mom in the morning for missing. He squinted at me and then. "Sai?"

"What are you doing up?" I repeated. Dad gave a weird look with a wry smile and made the bathroom sign with his knuckles. Oh. Right.

I nodded and tried to smile. "Okay, good night, Dad," I signed and left as quickly as I could. The bathroom door was adjacent to my room, so as I shut the door, I saw that Dad was still standing at the doorway, this time, he had twisted his back and was staring at me, but I couldn't see his eyes. I could only see his silhouette. Great. Any chance of me masturbating tonight with my DVD was all gone. I couldn't erase Dad's expression out of my head. I wanted to, but I couldn't. I shoved my DVD under my bed and thought of Emma. Within minutes, I was asleep.

I woke up with a jolt a few hours later and realized . . . I was completely turned on. The crotch of my pants looked like a tent. I looked over at the time and saw that it was 3:45 in the morning. Without thinking, I slid my hands down my pants and grasped the shaft of my penis. I felt my back stiffened, and then tried to relax. I didn't let myself think about anything else. My parents, Nick, my sister . . . anything. I let my mind go blank.

Well, no not really, because all of a sudden, I can only think of the facial expressions of the woman in the first DVD I watched. I hadn't seen the second one yet but I had firmly planted the first DVD in my mind so well.

I grasped my penis again, and then let go. I did this for several minutes, until I started going faster. I couldn't hear myself breathing, but I could tell I was breathing loudly. I couldn't stop. I didn't want to stop. I kept going and going until I rolled over to my side, my eyes squeezed shut, worrying if I had yelped out loud. Did you ever feel like you were just desperate to get somewhere and you keep running toward it, and when you finally got there it was a relief? That's how it felt. I had to go and wash my hands again. This time, it really needed to be washed.

I stood up, a little dizzy, a little spent. I, however, couldn't keep the grin off my face. Did I really do this? Yes, yes, I did. I made my promise to Nick! I stood up and ran to the door and yanked on the doorknob with my hand . . . the hand that I just used. Okay, so I can't be careless either. I wiped the doorknob with my shirt, and went to the bathroom. While washing my hands, I kept grinning. What an incredible feeling. I wonder how long it will take for me to do it again. And the best part? I still didn't watch the second DVD.

I became quite addicted to masturbating. I was convinced my parents knew, but I didn't care as much. I was concerned though, how loud I was becoming at night, so I started to shove a sock in my mouth to keep me from squealing. I noticed though, that I was salivating a lot during it, so I had to keep changing the sock every night. Nick was very impressed with my first experience with masturbation, and I had felt very comfortable in telling him how the first experience went.

Talking to Nick was very freeing. He had immediately, since the first day we met, assumed the role of the big brother that I so desperately needed. I felt like I could trust him with everything too, I can tell him how I felt, and I even felt that if I got mad or angry at him, our friendship wouldn't be severed. What a great feeling, having a friend I could lean on. I told him how I felt, I told him the things I wrote in my journal, and out of respect Nick never asked me to see what I had written inside the book.

With school projects, Nick helped me out. I found that Nick was particularly very good in math. Well, that is bit of an understatement. I had learned early on, that being good in math meant you were one day meant to be a doctor, an astronaut or a scientist. In my room, I had a poster of Marc Garneau, the first Canadian astronaut in space, and always wondered what it would be like to be *that* smart. I was not interested in math or sciences, and the stars had no effect on me, but I did have a poster of Marc Garneau up on my wall. It was so huge it covered almost the entire wall. Nick came over once for dinner and commented on it.

"I had no idea you were into astronomy," he signed. I shook my head.

"I am not at all," I signed back. "I just like Marc Garneau."

I had met Nick's girlfriend, Rachel, several times and I thought of how much I admired their relationship. I said so to Nick that evening, when we were sitting on the floor in my room. Nick's main purpose that night was to give me some more porn. I asked him if he ever wanted anything for it. Money? Nick had always given me the porn for free. Nick smiled and signed that he burned me copies and he wanted nothing from them at all. Nick, sitting on the floor, turned to me, I was lying on my bed and I turned over to my side to look at him.

"Have you ever had a girlfriend before, Simon?" Nick asked. I thought back to Nat, who I hadn't thought of or heard from in months. We hadn't gone back to that church, and for some reason, we never even ran into them in our small city. I signed that there was someone a long time ago. Thinking about Nat, I just realized, was not as hard as it used to be.

Nick looked like he wanted to ask a sensitive question but was waiting for the right way to ask me. I sat up and stared at him. He knew that this would annoy me. Nick was about to ask when a sudden turn of his head toward the door make me look toward the door too. Mom opened the door slightly and handed us cans of pop and a huge bowl of microwaved popcorn. I signed "thank you" and Mom shut the door again. Nick looked over and grinned at me. "The joys of living at home," he signed.

"What were you going to ask me?" I asked, impatient to get back on topic.

"I wanted to know, how interested are you in being in a relationship?" Nick all of a sudden started signing faster, but I understood everything he signed. He seemed to be more articulate when he was signing faster. "What are you looking for in a girl? Do they have to be deaf?"

I was shocked. I never thought about it before. Nick was still trying to get his thoughts out in sign language.

"It's just that, porn is great and everything, but nothing is better than the real thing," he signed. I lay back on my bed. Nick started to turn red.

It looked as if he had been wanting to ask me these questions for some time, but wasn't sure how to go about asking me.

"My last girlfriend wasn't deaf," I signed. Nick raised an eyebrow. "How did you communicate?" he asked. I shrugged.

"We didn't really. Mostly on notepads," I signed. Nick looked like he was dying to ask me a question. I knew what he wanted to know. I waited five minutes and when he didn't say anything, I smiled and signed. "I'm a virgin." Nick looked relieved that he didn't have to ask me. He nodded slowly.

"That was what you wanted to know?" I signed. Nick nodded. "Not just that. I also wanted to know if you would be interested in meeting a friend of mine and Rachel's. She's actually a friend of Rachel's cousin, who is studying in a community college nearby. Her name is Aimee. Very bright, very smart. She actually skipped a few grades and is already doing college courses."

This was way too much information in such a short amount of time. Yes, I watched porn and fantasized about the women in the movies, but I hadn't thought too much about women ever since Nat. Not that I was broken-hearted over her, but women just seemed safer in the DVDs. I could fantasize about them without having to worry if they would end up breaking my heart. I didn't say this to Nick at all. For some reason, I had a feeling Nick would laugh at me if I had said this to him.

"Would you be interested in meeting her?" Nick asked. I shrugged.

"Does she know anything about me?" I asked. "Anything about my disability?"

Nick nodded. "Yes, we already told her about you. She is interested in meeting you."

I gave him a look. "Really?"

"Yes. Rachel and I thought it would be nice if the four of us went on a double date, group thing." (Nick showed a look of grotesque at the words "double date.") "And we would see how things would turn out. Aimee already agreed to it."

"Aimee already agreed to it? Agreed to a double date with a deaf boy she has never met?" I signed skeptically. Nick looked a bit uncomfortable. "Well, we have been talking about you to her for some time now and she has been by the shop too. She thinks you're really cute." Nick stood up and started pacing back and forth, something that I noticed he did when he was trying to think. He often did this in the back when he was doing orders at the butcher shop.

"There's no harm in meeting her, Simon. Who knows?" He looked at me. "I kind of worry about you." I wanted to get mad, but I couldn't get mad. "Because I rather sit and watch porn than go out on dates?"

"Well, kind of, Simon, yes," Nick admitted. "Don't let your being deaf stop you from living. Who knows? Aimee may be your soul mate! Maybe she isn't. But you won't know if you don't give it a chance."

I thought about, and told Nick that I would think about it. Nick was respectful, and I had asked to see a picture of her, and Nick got mad at me. So I got mad back.

"Well, just because I'm deaf doesn't mean that my eyes don't work. I need to be attracted to her too!" Nick shot me a look of exasperation. "I never thought of you to be the shallow type, Simon!"

"How would you know? This is the first time you have ever tried to hook me up with a girl." I signed back furiously.

"Well, Simon, it shouldn't matter if she had three eyes and . . ." Nick then started to laugh.

I had noticed that Nick can't really sign when he is laughing really hard. "Okay, are you done?" I signed when he stopped laughing enough to open his eyes and look at me. Nick started laughing again. I waited patiently. I glanced at my watch.

"Okay, I'm done now," Nick signed.

"So will I get to see a picture?" I asked. Nick pulled out his phone and nodded. "I'll ask Rachel now," he finger-spelled, his other hand holding the phone.

I can't exactly say it was love at first sight, but Nick presented me with a picture of Aimee and Rachel the very next day just before our Saturday morning shift. She was absolutely beautiful. My breath caught back a bit and I suddenly felt a bit intimidated.

Nick was watching my reaction. I looked up at Nick, angry. "You made me think she was an ugly old hag!" I signed angrily. Nick had a smirk on his face. I started whacking him on his forearm. "Relax, Simon!" Nick stepped away from me and slipped his cell phone into the front pocket of his apron. "I just didn't want you to base this whole group date thing on looks," he signed. He raised his eyebrows. "Seems like you are interested!" I turned red. Aimee was beautiful. There was something about her smile. Her eyes. I glared at Nick. "You had me thinking she was ugly, and so it was okay to meet her. Now I know that she isn't, and she is beautiful, I am going to end up acting like a fool!" I signed.

Nick shook his head. "Where is your confidence?"

I took a deep breath. I had none. I mean, I was terrible with my social skills. I had anger management problems and this whole thing without me not being able to talk and hear . . . . it only worked around people who bothered to understand me. I thought back to all the students in my school who didn't know me or ever bothered to even know me. Although we had gone to the same school for years, I had no friends in high school. I only had my social worker Darah, my family and my friends at the butcher shop. Nick. I had Nick.

"I don't know if I have any," I signed to Nick. Nick shook his head. "I am not going to take that for an answer. You have a week to find out why Aimee asked to meet you in the first place, and then we are going out for coffee." Ew. Coffee. Who drinks coffee?

"I do. Most grown-ups do," Nick signed teasingly.

The following Saturday, I met Aimee. I have to say, the entire week, I was so nervous that I signed to my parents that Nick was introducing me to Aimee. My parents needed to know everything about her.

"I know nothing about her, and it is really just some of us going out for coffee. It's no big deal." Mom grinned at me. "And this is why you're nervous," Mom signed. I shrugged.

Emma looked over at me. "Is she pretty?" she signed. I nodded vigorously, then turned red. Dad smiled at me. "Just have fun and be yourself."

"Bring your notebooks!" Emma signed. I reeled from the idea of having to pass notes all evening to a girl who I found to be so beautiful. It was then that I started to cry. In front of my parents and my sister, I started to cry. Tears of frustration from the last couple of years, everything that I have been thinking of, everything that I have expressed in my journal. I was just tired.

"Why would you guys even bother to adopt a deaf boy?" I signed. Mom had immediately run to my side and instead of pushing her away, I collapsed in her arms My family is not the emotional, crying kind of family, not like a horrible after-school special, where we had thirty minutes to fix a huge family problem just before the credits went up. So crying in front of them was awkward, yet it wasn't. Dad didn't move from his seat, but his eyes were filled with concern. I appreciated it. Emma hadn't move from her seat either, and was staring at me with concern as well. Emma knew I was adopted, well, because it was also pretty obvious, since we didn't even come close to looking alike. However, it was never an issue with us. I never once addressed that it was tough to be adopted, and not know how to fit in, and how alone I felt most of the time, even though my family has been nothing but wonderful to me.

I wasn't complaining about being deaf, being deaf and mute was all I knew in my life, but it was at this very moment, just hours away from going on a date with someone, was when I realized just how different I truly was from the rest of the world. "How am I supposed to go on a date with someone and talk to her when she can't even speak sign language?" I signed when I sat up and wiped my nose across my sleeve. Emma jumped up and ran across the room to give me a box of tissue.

"Simon, you are worrying too much about this," Dad signed when he caught my eye. Mom nodded in agreement. "Didn't you say that she asked to meet you?"

I nodded slowly. Yes, this was true. She asked me to meet me knowing that I was deaf. "Why would she do that though? How are we supposed to communicate?"

Mom signed. "She knew that and she still wanted to meet you. This sounds like a really innocent thing, meeting up for coffee. I think you are thinking too much of it." I knew they wanted to understand, but they just didn't. Even I didn't understand how I was feeling inside. Dad looked at me, exasperated. "It's just coffee, Simon!"

It definitely was innocent enough. I was pleasantly surprised to see that I was not the only one who brought a pad of paper. Nick brought his own, Rachel brought a stack of paper and even a bag of pens, and Aimee had brought her own pad of paper. I was touched, and felt my face going warm. Aimee had the cap off the pen and was ready to write anything at any given moment. The attention my friends were giving me was nice. I hadn't expected everyone to have their own pads of paper, I had expected that I would be left out of most of the conversations.

Aimee wrote on a slip. "What kind of movies do you watch?" I smiled. I love horror movies. I absolutely love horror movies, and wrote down that I did. Aimee made a face at me and wrote, "You don't get nightmares?" I grinned.

"Of course I do," I wrote, "but that's the best part of it." Aimee flipped over a page in her notebook. "What is the best part?" I grinned, and grabbed her pad of paper. No point in wasting trees. Aimee and I exchanged a whole entire conversation with her pad of paper and half of mine; I didn't even realize that Rachel and Nick had stood up and left. I glanced up, startled. Aimee hadn't noticed either, she was busy answering the question I had asked about why she thought mutants should be free in the X-Men series. Nick, though, had left his pad of paper where he was sitting and I could see that he had written on the top of his pad of paper and folded it over.

I reached over and grabbed the pad and quickly checked what Nick wrote. I smiled. Nick wrote, "Guess you didn't need us after all."

I looked at Aimee who was smiling at me. She gestured to the seats where Rachel and Nick were sitting, and then shrugged. I smiled, hesitating. Then I showed Aimee what Nick had written. Aimee blushed. I blushed too, thinking in my head that I had never seen anything prettier. I looked down, overwhelmed with how quickly my heart was beating. A few seconds later, I felt Aimee's hand go on top of mine. Slowly I looked up and grinned. Aimee shoved the pad of paper over to me.

"Do you want to come over to my place and watch some horror movies?" she had written.

"Which ones do you have?" I wrote back.

"None, we would have to go by a Blockbuster and pick one up," she wrote back.

I nodded. "Let's go!" I picked up my cell phone and texted my parents that I would be going to Aimee's house. Mom immediately texted back, asking where Aimee lived. I showed Aimee the text, and she carefully texted her address and home number. The light on my cell suddenly lit while Aimee was texting my mom her address. Aimee passed over the phone saying something, and then stopped abruptly when she realized that she was talking out loud. She pointed to the phone, a little icon on the phone saying that my dad had texted me too. I opened the text from my dad.

"Don't stay out too late, and call me to pick you up. Happy face." (Yes, my dad did write out the words. "Happy Face." He thinks it's funny. It really isn't anymore.)

Aimee had been writing on the pad of paper while I was responding to my dad, and passed me the note when I looked up at her. Aimee had written. "There is a Blockbuster just fifteen minutes away from my house. We have to walk by my house first to get to the Blockbuster from here, if you don't mind the walk."

"I don't have a rental card," I wrote. Aimee grinned at me and pulled hers out of her wallet.

I paid for our coffee (including Nick and Aimee's) and I held the door open for Aimee. Aimee walked out and then paused as I walked through the door. I almost ran into her. I can tell that Aimee had felt bad that she had her back toward me. I fell into step beside her and my left hand brushed right up beside hers. (I saw this in a movie once that if you keep brushing your hand right up beside the girl you like, she'll eventually take a hint and grab your hand.) It was true, it didn't take long. After the second brush, Aimee grabbed my hand. I was thrilled, but I could feel my heart pounding like crazy. It was awkward, I didn't know how to hold her hand, and I was suddenly aware that my hand started to sweat. Or was it Aimee's? I hoped it was Aimee's. Partly due to the fact that we couldn't talk while walking, I was relieved that we couldn't communicate during the walk. Every once in a while, Aimee squeezed my hand reassuringly, quite possibly because she can feel me tense up with nervousness.

After twenty minutes, we walked by a small well-kept house, and Aimee stopped slightly and pointed to herself and then to the house. I nodded understandingly, and then Aimee pointed down the street. Squinting, I could see the blue and yellow Blockbuster sign. Walking quietly, sometimes our sides hitting, I found my hand starting to relax in her grip. I thought of her. Aimee. I snuck a glance over to her, which she caught immediately, and smiled at me. Embarrassed that she caught me admiring her, I looked straight ahead, but felt Aimee's eyes still on me. I kept looking straight ahead. Suddenly, I felt her tug at my arm; pretending to not notice, I kept looking straight ahead. Aimee tugged harder. Trying really hard to not smile or show any signs of emotions on my face, I kept staring straight ahead. I hopped up on the curb and then jumped back down. Aimee tugged at my hand again. I continued to ignore her, trying very hard to keep the smile off my face. Aimee tugged again. I kept my hand tightly around her hand but still ignored her. Aimee stopped tugging. I glanced over at her and saw that she too was smiling.

We walked in silence for a few more minutes. Then I tugged her arm. That was all it took for Aimee to start laughing hysterically. I don't think I have ever seen anything more beautiful than her smile. I ignored her laughing as I had realized, we both refused to let go of each other's hands. In fact, we both ended up twining our fingers. I laughed, suddenly realizing that my heart had started to beat differently. Reaching the Blockbuster, I knew then and there, I didn't want this night to ever end.

I hadn't been to this Blockbuster, and Aimee had never gone to the Horror section of this Blockbuster, so Aimee had to ask one of the guys

who worked there. Aimee found out where the section was but wrote on
the pad of paper that I could pick whatever I wanted and she will browse
through other movies. I didn't want to let go of her hand, and I could feel
her hesitation in letting go of mine, but we eventually let go. I decided to
pick a ghost/thriller movie that I had seen many times, one with Kevin
Bacon in it, and quickly got Aimee so we could rent it. As soon as we
stepped outside the store, we immediately grabbed hands again. Safe.

We didn't push each other around when we were walking back to
Aimee's house. I wanted to, but since Aimee didn't initiate it, I didn't
either. I was sort of afraid though of Aimee feeling how warm my hands
were, almost convinced that she can feel my heart racing through my
palm. I definitely can feel something pulsating but wasn't sure if it was
Aimee's palm or mine.

Aimee immediately stuck a package of microwaved popcorn, and
while I was setting up the movie in the living room, she passed a note from
the notepad that said, "My parents are divorced. It's just me and my mom.
My older sister moved out a few years ago, and we don't talk much."
With that, she disappeared, and I could smell the buttery scent of popcorn.
Normally, the scent of popcorn would make me gag, but tonight I didn't
seem to mind it. I didn't plan on eating any though. I don't like how the
kernels always get stuck in my teeth. One time one kernel got stuck, and it
took four toothpicks, Dad, and half a foot of floss to get it out.

Aimee set up the DVD so that there were subtitles but thought it
was funny when she set it up in Spanish. I thought it was funny when
I realized that I understood a few words. I didn't flinch during the
Spanish subtitles, and although I didn't understand word for word what
was written, I got the gist of it. Aimee sat there staring at me. Finally,
she wrote on the pad, "You know how to read Spanish?" I took the pen
from her and wrote, "My dad is from Costa Rica." Aimee read this and
cocked her head to the side. I can tell she was confused. I was beginning
to get confused too. I wrote, "I'm adopted."

Aimee turned bright red and took the pen from me so I couldn't see
she was embarrassed. "I know. I just don't know where Costa Rica is."
I paused, realizing that I didn't know either. I shrugged and waved my
hand, indicating that it was no big deal and then took the remote and
changed the subtitles for English then went back to the first scene so
I can understand it again. Aimee settled in deeper into the couch, right
beside me, and grabbed my hand again. On her other hand, she held the
notepad and pen ready.

I thought Rachel and Nick were going to pounce on me the next morning when they showed up at my house. Dad let them in saying that he was going to make a huge Sunday breakfast. Mom was smiling so much that I refused to make eye contact with me, but Emma had no shame in smiling at me openly. I was a little embarrassed, but knew that I would have to explain the full details of my date with Aimee eventually.

"How was it?" Dad signed, grinning. Dad had been home sleeping on the couch when I came home. As soon as I saw my dad sleeping on the couch, I immediately thought that Mom and Dad had a fight. Although I had never seen them fight to the point where they didn't sleep in the same bed, I've seen it on television, so I thought maybe that is what had happened. Then I saw someone else stir on the other couch and saw that Emma had fallen asleep too. They were eagerly waiting to know about my date with Aimee. I tiptoed past them both, too much in a good mood to get upset at this intrusiveness, but as soon as I walked past the couch Emma was asleep in, I saw Mom sitting in the kitchen table, drinking something very warm, because I can see the steam vividly coming from the mug. Mom smiled at me and motioned for me to come into the kitchen. I came over to her and kissed her on the cheek.

"Did you have a good night?" Mom signed. I nodded, my face turning red. Mom grinned.

"I'm glad. Go to bed. Emma and Dad were waiting for you, but they can wait until tomorrow morning." I nodded, feeling my shoulders relax. I kissed Mom again on the cheek and signed "Good night."

"Good night, Sai," Mom signed back, smiling. As I walked out of the kitchen, I couldn't help but think that Mom's eyes looked a little sad.

Dad cooked pancakes for breakfast. There was a stack of them, yet three empty boxes of pancake mix was sitting on the counter. Mom followed my gaze and pointed to the garbage. I looked inside and saw that Dad had burned, quite possibly, two-and-a-half boxes.

"It was good," I signed. Rachel and Nick were already eating with Emma, and

Mom was brewing a cup of coffee. "We left early," Nick explained to my parents, with a twinkle in his eye. "Simon didn't need us." I blushed. Rachel looked over at me and smiled, then writing on the dry erase board, she wrote, "Aimee texted me when you left last night. She said she had a good time." I blushed again. I thought back to the night before, and how the evening was wonderfully perfect. Aimee and I had held hands the entire time during the movie. She had her eyes shut for most of the movie, and I saw her reach out and hit the mute button at the very beginning. So basically, she hardly watched the movie. I didn't close my eyes once, I loved it. This has always been one of my favorite horror movies. I kept my eyes glued to the subtitles, afraid to move my eyes even for a minute. When the movie ended, Aimee quickly kissed me on the cheek. Then I said good night and walked home, texting my parents that I was on the way home.

"Sounds boring," Emma signed. Mom gave a huge look of surprise and Dad threw his head back and laughed. Nick grinned. "When are you guys seeing each other again?" he signed. I finger-spelled back. "T-o-n-i-g-h-t." I smiled.

Nick pressed for more information during work that day. Sadly enough, Emma was right, it really was boring. I explained the story over and over again to Nick, not really telling him too much of the walk over to the Blockbuster, as that was my favorite part of the evening. In fact, no one asked for information about the walk because I guess that was basically what it was. A walk to Blockbuster. I knew though, that Aimee and I had an unspoken agreement that the walk over to Blockbuster and the walk to back to her house was the best part. Knowing that I wasn't pressured to communicate, but was speaking volumes anyways, was nice. I knew from the way Aimee had held my hand, from how she squeezed it from time to time, how massive my hand seemed compared to hers, yet it was still a perfect fit; it was really nice.

"No action." Nick shook his head signing, then started packing sausages into plastic bags. I pretended I didn't see him sign, but I knew he caught my smile.

Chapter 7

Aimee and I planned to see each other every single night that week. Although we did the same thing—walk to Blockbuster, pick a horror movie, Aimee watched it through her eyelids and with the mute button off, and I kept my eyes glued to the screen—it was heaven. I think Aimee was relieved that she didn't have to discuss the movie with me, she knew I knew she didn't pay attention, and I didn't mind. Every single night ended with a kiss on her part, quickly on my cheek, and then me waving good bye and then leaving. Every time I turned around, Aimee was watching me from the door. I always turned around already halfway down the driveway to wave again. Every night I came home, Dad was sleeping on the couch with Emma on the other couch and Mom was doing some sort of motherly activity in the kitchen table. One evening she was sewing pillow cases. The next evening she was doing a word search. The evening after that, she was making jam. I came into the kitchen and saw about twenty jars of already filled reddish pink goop.

"Jam? Since when did you ever make Jam?" I signed.

"When there's a sale of rotten strawberries at the Farmers Market." Mom wrote on the dry erase born because she didn't know how to sign "rotten," "strawberries," and "Farmers Market."

"These are all spoiled strawberries?" I signed. Mom nodded.

"I am not eating that!" I signed, slightly outraged. Mom sighed, stretched and got the dry erase maker. "None of us are. We are giving them away from Christmas." I laughed and got another marker to write. "Mom, that's terrible." Mom laughed too and wrote, "Dad liked them. He had three pieces of toast with this jam for dinner. Emma had a slice. If they can eat it and are still alive, I am sure they're good to give away."

I chuckled and shook my head. I was about to walk out of the kitchen when suddenly Mom's hand stopped me. I turned around.

"How is Aimee?" Mom signed.

I nodded. "Very good."

"What movie did you watch tonight?" Mom signed.

"*The Ring.*"

"What was that about?"

I yawned and picked up the marker. I started to erase the previous notes and wrote, "Dead girl comes back to life through a well." Then I turned around and made a face at Mom. Mom's face looked disgusted.

"Really, Simon" She shook her head. "I can't believe you watch things like that. How does Aimee feel about it?"

"She doesn't really watch the movie," I signed. "She turns on the mute button and squeezes her eyes shut the entire time."

Mom looked a bit skeptical. "Really?"

"Really."

"You guys just watch the movie?" Mom signed.

I nodded, feeling my face turn red. Was there something wrong with me? Were we supposed to do something else? I signed this to Mom, who suddenly looked very uncomfortable.

"Well, no, Simon, but you're a . . ." I raised my eyebrows and cocked my head to one side.

"Deaf?" I signed, feeling my blood rise. Mom looked at me dead in the eye when I signed this.

"Simon, can you relax. I meant, you are a *boy*. A *teen*." I gave her a look of defiance.

"So?" I slammed my fist unto the kitchen table and the jars of jam rattled. I slammed it again and one of the jars fell over. Mom started to look frustrated. Like she hadn't planned on having this conversation. She started to talk, but I couldn't read her lips. I shook my head, and Mom caught herself. All of a sudden, she looked up and was staring over my shoulder. I turned around and saw Dad standing there. Looking confused and completely bewildered, he started to talk, but the kitchen was too dark for me to read his lips. I stood out of the way, off to one side, so I can read both their conversations.

"What is going on?" Dad signed. Mom looked terrified of my anger. "I wanted to talk to Simon about sex," she signed meekly.

Dad looked like he was ready to laugh and then swallowed it. I looked at Mom with a surprised look. "You did?" I signed, feeling my face burn.

"Of course, Simon. Now that you have a girlfriend, I just want you to be prepared." Dad finally laughed. "Simon, what did you think your mother wanted to talk to you about?"

I shrugged, looking down. I looked up at Dad and signed. "I didn't know she wanted to talk to me." Dad gave me a look and pointed to the jars of jam. "You think Mom is doing this for fun?" No one had bothered to pick up the one that fell over when I was slamming the table and the jam started to pour out. Dad leaned over and set it up right, and then dipped his finger into the jam on the table. "It is not very good jam" He signed. I laughed. Mom was still backed up, her hands clasped in front of her afraid. Her wide eyes looked at me and I immediately felt terrible. I looked at Mom and signed. "I'm sorry."

Mom's face immediately relaxed. "It's okay," Dad signed. "We can talk about this tomorrow." Dad looked over at me and smiled. "Did you have a good night?" I nodded.

"What did you watch tonight?" Dad signed.

"*The Ring.*"

Dad nodded. "That's a good one. One of my favorites"

The next morning, Dad signed that he would drive me to school. I was surprised. Dad usually leaves really early for work because the parking is so expensive where he works. If he leaves half an hour earlier, he could find parking on the street and wouldn't have to pay for parking. I grabbed a piece of toast and shook my head when Mom handed me a jar of jam, kissed her on her cheek and Emma goodbye, and went outside with Dad.

"You might have to pay for parking," I signed to Dad. "I took the day off," Dad signed.

"You did?"

"Yeah. After school, are you going over to Aimee's?" Dad signed.

"I nodded."

Dad nodded back. "Do you think you can get away with coming out for lunch with me then?"

I shrugged. "You're the parent. You just have to talk to the school," I signed.

Dad looked embarrassed. "Right. I'm the parent," he signed.

"If you park on the side at the visitors parking, you can go and talk to the school. I have a free period after lunch, so I get a whole hour and forty-five minutes off," I signed. Dad looked relieved with this news and parked in the visitor's parking.

Dad told the school he was going to take me out for lunch and promised he would be in front of the school when lunch began. I texted Nick immediately to let him know that I was having lunch with my dad and that we may be having "the talk." I laughed when I sent the text and Nick immediately replied. "Awkward!"

I texted back. "Both my parents are acting weird," Nick replied. "They're just being parents. Enjoy it. Please let me know how your Dad tells you about sex. I bet there's going to be a lot of acting involved!"

I thought about it all morning. I thought back to Aimee and couldn't help but smile. I thought about her smile, her hand in mine, her . . . *rap, rap, rap* . . . I looked up and saw my science teacher, Miss Bishop, smile at me. One of the few teachers in my school who could sign to me. "Everything okay, Simon?" she signed and spoke at the same time. I blushed and nodded, looking up at her. I smiled and picked up my pen, copying the notes again from the board again. Miss Bishop went back to the board and half-sat on her desk, ready to sign and talk at the same time.

Lunch finally came and I texted my dad, who texted back to say he was waiting outside. I wasn't worried about talking to Dad about sex. I was curious as to how he would explain it—or should I just let him know about the books I have been reading? Before leaving the school, I stopped by my locker and pulled out two pads of paper and a couple of colored pens. I may not need them, but Dad may.

Dad waved at me when he saw me come out, he was leaning on the car. I grinned, happy to see him and waved back.

"Having a good morning?" he signed as I buckled my seatbelt. I only caught half of his sign and asked him to repeat it.

"Having a good morning?" he signed again, smiling. I noticed that he seemed nervous. He wouldn't look at me in the eye, which is odd for my dad who makes a point to look straight into my eyes when signing. Dad put the car into gear and I signed to him on where we were going for lunch.

Dad made a gesture. "It's up to you," he signed. But he was heading a specific road that served his favorite fish and chips.

"Caity's Fish and Chips," I signed. Dad grinned and nodded, just as he pulled into the parking lot.

"Are you going to talk to me about sex?" I signed after we had done our order. Dad looked nervous, and shook his head slightly. I gave him a look and took out the pads of paper and the pens. Dad didn't know what to say, but he burst out laughing. He started laughing so hard, tears started to fall from his face. I didn't find it funny, but I grinned. Dad tried to catch his breath, took a deep breath, and then focused on a spot on the floor. Then his shoulders started shaking again, and he kept his laughter and started laughing through his nose. I took the pad of paper and wrote, "It's not that funny." For some reason, Dad found this extremely funny as well and burst out laughing again.

I smiled politely, and diverted my eyes, trying hard not to laugh as well. The waiter came by grinning and put our lunch on the table. I looked up at him and he said something, but said it so quickly that I couldn't read his lips. I signed that I couldn't hear what he was saying and he nodded understandably and looked at Dad, who had regained himself and told him that I was deaf. The waiter smiled at me and all of a sudden his gestures became huge. He pointed to the ketchup and I nodded and also pointed to more napkins. It felt like a ridiculous game of charades. Dad had this look on his face where he seemed like he was trying really hard to hold his laughter in. Not the brightest crayon in the box, because he thought drinking a sip of his Coke would help him stop laughing. I caught his eye, and he burst out laughing inside the glass and Coke splattered everywhere. I couldn't keep my laughter in at all, and started laughing too. Dad was contagious and I guess I was too, because it made the waiter laugh. Other customers having lunch looked over us and smiled. I stopped laughing first and wrote on the notepad. "I'm hungry now." and showed it to both the waiter and Dad and dug in.

I saw from the corner of my eye that Dad was talking to the waiter, and then a few minutes later, the waiter smiled at me and left. I looked up at Dad, and wrote on the notepad. "Did you want to talk about sex?" I asked. Dad shook his head but handed me a box that he was carrying in his jacket pocket. A box. I looked at it and picked it up. I laughed embarrassingly.

"C-o-n-d-o . . ." I finger spelled and Dad waved me away. I put my hand down and picked up a french fry. Dad refused to look at me in the eye, but stuffed his mouth with a big piece of halibut and then grabbed the pad of paper and a pen.

"You're a smart boy. We don't have to talk about it. Just wear these."

Mom was livid when she found out about our conversation during lunch. I don't think Dad had planned on telling her what had happened between during lunch, only that she knew we were having lunch together. But Dad had seen the neighbor outside and was talking to him after he picked me up after school and I just went into the house. Mom was sitting on the kitchen table with Emma, who was doing her math homework. Mom had an abacus out and also a calculator. I found this funny, as Emma is only in grade two.

"Calculator?" I smirked at Mom, who looked up with a smile when she saw me come in. Mom made a face at me and signed. "Math is harder nowadays!" I grinned.

"Where's Dad?" Mom signed.

"Outside, talking to Mr. Levy," I signed back, indicating to the window.

"How was lunch with Dad?" Mom signed. I reached into my knapsack and showed her the box of condoms Dad picked out for me. Mom's eyes grew big and slapped me on the wrist, nodding her chin toward Emma.

I shrugged. I dropped the box inside the bag and pulled out the notepad where Dad and I had the "talk" and went upstairs to my bedroom. Climbing up the stairs, I saw the lights flick on and off and Mom was standing at the bottom of the stairs.

"Dinner in an hour," she signed. I nodded. I was tired. I wanted to lie down for a little bit, but before lying down, I pulled out the box of condoms. I didn't open it, just held the box. I hadn't heard from Aimee all day but she had texted me saying that her sister was in town for a few days and wanted to spend time with her. I rolled over to my stomach and tried to close my eyes, but I couldn't relax. I thought of Aimee's smile again and looked at my hand, feeling her hand in mine. I smiled, thinking of her hand in mine, and felt drowsy. I fell asleep and woke up half an hour later to see Emma lying down beside me, her big green eyes looking right at me.

I sat up startled and signed. "What time is it?"

Emma held up eight fingers. I had fallen asleep for two hours.

"No dinner?" I signed, sitting up. I stretched and my eye caught the box of condoms on the pillow.

"Mommy and Daddy are fighting downstairs," Emma signed. I asked her to repeat her sign. Emma repeated and then started to cry.

"About what?" I signed.

"Your lunch with Daddy," Emma signed, mouthing the words. I looked at Emma and lay back down. Of course they did.

Emma snuggled up beside me and I wrapped an arm around my sister. I realized that she was shaking, and sat up. "Are you okay?" I signed, surprised at how hard she was shaking. Emma shook her head slowly and started to cry.

"What were they saying?" I signed. It was then that the lights in my room flicked on and I looked up to see Dad standing at the doorway. His eyes were filled with remorse.

"Dad, are you okay?" I signed. "Is everything okay?"

Dad nodded, smiling faintly. "Mom is mad that I didn't exactly talk to you about being a man." He walked over to my bed and sat on the edge. Emma crawled over and lay on Dad's lap. Dad looked at me and smiled. "She wanted me to really explain about everything, and is not too happy that I bought you a box of condoms."

I shrugged. "Did she not want me to wear them?" I signed.

Dad looked at me quizzically and signed. "No, Simon, she doesn't encourage you having sex."

"Where is Mom?" I signed.

"She left for a bit. I think she went to a twenty-four-hour grocery store. She's very upset with me," Dad signed. He hugged Emma, who wrapped her arms around his neck. Dad didn't move for a minute, then looked at me, and holding Emma, he signed. "I don't think it was wrong to give you the condoms. But your mother thinks I am not being a real parent." His eyes flashed with anger when he signed. "real."

I just stared at him, as I really didn't know what to think. I think Dad did the right thing. I think Dad read my mind, as he looked at me and signed. "You're going to have sex. It's human nature. Especially as a teen boy."

I nodded. "I hope so." Dad fought to keep the smile off his face and forced himself to become serious again.

"What made Mom so mad though?" I signed. Dad sighed and looked at me. He glanced down at Emma and saw that Emma had fallen asleep with her arms wrapped tightly around his neck, so Dad let go to sign. "Mom doesn't think I should have encouraged you having sex with Aimee."

"Dad, Aimee and I just met."

Dad nodded slowly. "I know. But I'm just saying that you're a teen boy, and this is something that you need to experience in life. I said this to your mother and that was when she got really upset with me." Dad looked remorseful. "Your mother and I are from two very different backgrounds. She had a brother who died of HIV when she was younger and she was very close to him. Her brother was very sexually active, so . . ."

Dad looked helpless and let his hands drop. Emma felt this and stirred but didn't wake up. "Mom is very sensitive about you being sexually active," he finally signed. Dad looked beaten. "I am sorry, but your mother is right."

I sighed and rolled my eyes. "I just met Aimee, Dad. And I would like some dinner." Sometimes I think my parents take this parenting thing too seriously.

Mom came home an hour later, while Dad and I were just cleaning up the dishes. I had my back toward the entrance, wiping the dishes. Mom was carrying several plastic bags. She looked at me and gave me a half-smile, but I looked away. She came over to me and tapped me on the shoulder. I didn't move, and I refused to look at her. I felt Mom looked down, and she slightly rubbed my back and turned around.

I wasn't too sure why I was mad at her. I felt like my parents were a little bit too involved with everything that was going on with me and Aimee. I just wanted them to back off. It is already hard enough having to deal with a relationship with someone than to deal with the whole situation with my parents. It seemed like they were just trying a little bit too hard to be involved with my life. I needed to tell them to back off.

In the middle of the night, I went downstairs to the kitchen and wiped the erase board clean. I scrummaged through a plastic bin where we kept the markers that were here and looked for a bright red marker. When I found the marker, I wrote in big letters. "Mom and Dad, I love you both, but please back off. Si."

I also drew a smiley face for Emma, just in case she felt left out. Then I went back to bed, with the intention of waking earlier than my parents and being out of the house when they got the note. That night, at dinner, no one said anything to me. But Emma had drawn a heart around my note.

Chapter 8

It was easy to write to Aimee about everything that is going on in my house. We have started writing a lot to each other; mostly everything we communicate is written through thick notebooks. We have also started sharing notebooks with each other. When I first told Aimee of how my parents were acting, she turned bright red. We never really looked at each other when we wrote about how my parents were acting. After passing the notebook back and forth, Aimee took the leap when she wrote, "How do you feel about sex?"

When she slid the notebook over to me, she idly picked up a french fry, popped it into her mouth, and idly flipped a page over a magazine. I can feel the tension though, as my pen paused over the notebook. I was startled. I glanced up at Aimee, who purposely kept her eyes glued to her magazine. She was focused on a deodorant ad. I kicked her under the table, but she still refused to look up at me. But I hinted a glimpse of a smile. I took a deep breath and wrote,

"How do you think I feel about it?" After a pause, I added a happy face. I slid the notebook over to Aimee, my face burning.

This time, Aimee didn't wait to write. She still refused to look up at me when she quickly jotted something down and practically shoved the notebook over to me. Glancing at what she wrote, I looked up, and she was smiling shyly at me. I reached over and grabbed her hand. That night, Aimee and I made love.

Over the course of the next few months, Aimee and I became sexually active. I was quite surprised at how amazing the feeling felt. It seemed that every time Aimee and I were together, we made love. I told Nick about it, who seemed uncomfortable that I was so open about how I felt about Aimee. I asked Nick about him and Rachel, and Nick refused to say anything.

"That's not cool, man," he signed. "Respect your girl if you love her. Learn to keep some things private."

I was ashamed when Nick signed this to me. "I'm sorry, I didn't know." I hung my head. I was just so happy to have been with someone who meant so much to me, who accepted me for who I was that I was surprised that the whole world didn't know how I felt. I felt like my heart was bursting with happiness. I thought about Aimee every second of the day. I was always thinking of her, and every time I did, I felt my heart was going to burst of happiness. Aimee and I spent every single day together, and the moments when we were not together, we were texting each other, writing e-mails, and trying some way to spend time together.

Aimee and I never fought, as it seemed as if she was having problems in other areas of her life. Aimee didn't get along with her mother at all, and her mother didn't seem to like the fact that she was dating me. In fact, I met her a few times, and she barely looked at me, and when she did, I could read her face loud and clear. Disgust. I didn't mind, though, as Aimee didn't seem at all affected by the fact that her mother hated me. As much as Aimee's mother showed remorse for me, she never told Aimee to stop seeing me. Or did she?

"She asked me a few times if there were other boys I was interested in," Aimee wrote in the notebook when I asked her this one evening after making love in her room. I felt a pang of jealousy.

"Other boys?" Aimee nodded and wrote, "I said no, and there never will be." Seeing these words made me feel like I was drowning in love, and I wrapped my arms around her. I felt myself harden, and so did Aimee. We made love again.

My parents are not stupid. Ever since I had asked that they back off, they had done so wonderfully. Every day they asked how Aimee was doing, but they have backed off completely with everything else. A mother knows, though, and one morning before school, I caught her looking at me. It was the way I was looking at her. I cocked my head to one side, my way of asking, "What's up?" Mom continued to look at me, with a smile that I couldn't quite comprehend. Just then, Dad walked in with Emma on his back. Instinctively, Dad knew that he walked into a moment. It's not every day you see your wife and son staring at each other in the kitchen. Dad pretended to not notice and grabbed an apple, tossed it into the air, and, much to Emma's delight, caught it with his teeth. Emma laughed, jumped off Dad's back, and ran into me. I knelt down and gave her a hug. I glanced over at Mom who went back to putting the groceries away. She turned her back toward us. Dad looked at me and made a face, pointing his chin toward Mom. I shrugged.

At that moment, Mom had turned around and saw the charade Dad and I were playing. Emma caught this and hid her giggle behind a fist. Mom signed, "What's going on?" to Dad and me. I shrugged.

"Nothing." Dad smiled at me, winking. Mom gave Dad a look, and I knew at that moment, that Mom and Dad knew how close Aimee and I had gotten. It was the way she looked at Dad, and the way Dad glanced at me. I raised my hand to sign. "Am I being paranoid, or do you guys know something?" Mom and Dad spoke with their eyes, and Mom glanced down at Emma, who was closely watching the silent conversation we were all having. I saw Mom's lips move and her hand stretched out. Emma jumped off the kitchen chair and grabbed Mom's hand, who led her out of the kitchen. I faced Dad. Dad looked at me dead in the eye.

"How are things with Aimee?" he signed. He refused to take his eyes off of me. I smiled and stared at him straight back.

"Very well, thank you for asking," I signed with a grin. Dad paused, his hands half-raised. Then he plunged in, signing quickly. "Are you both using protection?"

I caught my breath. Of course not. I have never worn protection since Aimee and I became intimate. One look at my face and Dad knew. I immediately felt defensive and signed. "Aimee and I are not sleeping around," I signed angrily. "We are only together with each other."

Dad's face darkened. "I'm not talking about that!" He signed furiously. "What if Aimee got pregnant? Is she on birth control?" Pregnant? Pregnant? Pregnant? A little alien inside the belly? A bun in the oven? That kind of pregnant? I was shocked. I didn't even think about that.

Dad grabbed a marker from the bin and wrote on the dry erase board. "Is Aimee on birth control?" I shook my head slowly, not to answer "no" but to answer. "I have no idea." Dad knew this and sighed.

"Simon, you need to know these things. She has never mentioned that she was on birth control with you?" I shook my head. I thought wearing protection was to not get a disease. I have no idea why the thought of not getting Aimee pregnant had not crossed my mind. Suddenly, I was furious with Aimee. "Aimee never said anything to me! Isn't that her job too?"

Dad looked at me, with an exasperated look on his face. "It is both your jobs!" He wrote on the board. He was so angry that he spelled "jobs" without an "o." I pointed this out and Dad slapped his hand on the table. I quickly grabbed my cell phone out of my pocket and messaged Aimee. "Are you on birth control?" Dad slapped his hand on the table again, angry that I had stopped watching him lecture me. I held my hand out to say, "Hold on," and Dad put his hand on his waist and waited for me to put my phone down.

"Simon, if you are going to be sexually active, you need to be very careful!" My hands started to shake and I couldn't sign properly. I was so angry and frustrated. At whom? I don't know.

At that moment, I saw my phone blink and I grabbed it to read Aimee's single message.

"No." I felt my eyes grow huge and all of a sudden my heart started to thump. I thought my heart was going to jump out of my chest.

"Dad, Aimee is not on birth control," I signed slowly. Dad took a deep breath and opened his mouth to say something, then realized he was talking to me. He placed the marker on the table and signed slowly. "You need to wear condoms. You can get Aimee pregnant." Condoms? Those things felt uncomfortable!

"You can't really feel anything when you are wearing condoms," I signed matter-of-factly.

Dad pounded his fist on the table. "You are seventeen years old! What are you going to do if you accidentally get Aimee pregnant?" I shrugged. "I'll tell her to go on birth control." With that, I grabbed my jacket and my cell phone from the kitchen table and left the house to see Aimee.

I knocked on Aimee's door after texting her that I would be at her house in a minute. She was already sitting on the front porch when I came. I realized that I had left the notebook we were recently using at home. Aimee greeted me with a huge smile and a hug and then ran inside to grab a spare notebook. She came out of the house ripping pages off an old spiral and handed me a pen. Before handing me the notebook though, she wrote, "Why did you ask me if I was on birth control?"

"My parents found out we were intimate," I wrote. "And I didn't lie. I told my dad we weren't using any protection, any condoms, and he asked me if you were on birth control."

Aimee looked down and blushed. I continued writing. "Why are you not on birth control? Should we get you some? Are you not scared of being pregnant?" I put the notebook in her hands and Aimee looked down. She sat on the steps of her veranda and I sat down next to her. I suddenly saw her hands were shaking. I all of a sudden had a sinking feeling in my stomach. I didn't move. I waited for Aimee to write something.

Finally . . . *finally*, she wrote, "I missed my period the last two months." This didn't mean anything to me and wrote that. "What does that mean?"

"It means I think I'm pregnant," she wrote.

Have you ever felt your heart stop? I did. And it lasted for a whole two minutes. I think I blanked out completely after that. I know I passed out, fell on the floor and fainted. I just remember reading the words on the notebook and then my head hitting the pavement. I woke up to someone hitting my face, and it was Mom and Dad. Aimee was standing beside me, her eyes bugged out. Dad was kneeling next to me, and Mom was the one who was slapping my face. I saw Mom's mouth move, mouthing *"Simon!"* When they saw that I had opened my eyes, Dad pulled me up to a sitting position. I looked around.

"Where is Emma?" I signed. My head hurt. Aimee ran inside the house and came out with a package of frozen ground meat. I touched the side of my head where I felt a huge bump. Mom placed the frozen meat on my head and Aimee ran back inside and came out with a bottle of cold water.

"What happened?" I signed. I shook my head slowly. Mom signed. "You fainted. You had passed out for fifteen minutes. Aimee called us."

"I fainted? How?" I signed. Dad looked at Mom and signed. "You heard some bad news and couldn't take it." Dad said this while signing to me and I saw Aimee flinch and turn red.

"What bad news?" I signed. Mom sat me up and I moved over to the steps on the front porch. Dad sat next to me. Aimee stood there awkwardly. Dad motioned for her to sit down beside me, but she shook her head. I saw her lips move. "I'm fine, thanks." I saw Mom turn to Aimee, so I couldn't read her lips. Aimee nodded slowly and picked up the notebook. Mom handed her a pen from her purse and I watched as Aimee glanced at me, taking a deep breath and wrote something on the notebook. She slowly handed it to me, and I turned it around, without taking my eyes off of her. I could sense absolute fear in her eyes.

"I am pregnant," she had written in block letters. I felt my head fall toward the pavement again, but I felt a large hand cup my head just before it hit the ground. Good old Dad.

Chapter 9

Aimee was three months pregnant. I don't think I have ever felt so scared and terrified my entire life. Aimee cried, and Mom hugged her that evening, telling her that she can sleep over at our place because Aimee had not told her mom about the baby yet. She wanted to tell me. Ironically, the day Dad confronted me about wearing protection was the day Aimee found out she was pregnant. I asked my parents if they knew anything before, but they both denied it.

It always struck me as funny how they seemed to know that day that Aimee and I were sexually active. Later, when our baby Quinn was born and I was carrying her, I thought back to that moment when my parents seemed to know me so well. It always makes me smile. My entire life, I have always wondered if my parents knew me, if they understood me, with me being adopted and our weird communication style. But I guess deep down, they did know me. They knew me very well.

Aimee's mother kicked her out the following week when we told her. Aimee asked that my mom come with us and I have never seen such an angry woman my entire life. It was at that moment that I was very happy I couldn't hear what they were saying, because Aimee's mother was so expressive, screaming with her eyes wild, lunging toward Aimee as if to strangle her. Mom and I had to pull Aimee back and Mom bravely stood in front of Aimee and me. Every time I saw Aimee's mother's mouth open in a crazy rage, I felt Aimee squeeze my hand. With all the screaming, Aimee completely forgot that I couldn't hear a word of what her mother was saying, and I didn't bother to try to read her lips. I kept my eyes to the floor, and would once in a while kick my foot into the ground.

Aimee's mother stomped upstairs and Mom turned to us, her eyes weary, as if she just won a battle. She was crying, as her eyes were red. I suddenly felt so bad for her and reached over to give her a hug. Both my parents have been supportive ever since they screamed at me for being irresponsible the night I fainted twice. It was a horrid week. I wanted to run away. I didn't know what to say to Aimee, who looked terrified and confused.

The topic of abortion eventually came up, and both my parents seemed to have spoken about it before presenting it to me. After having it drawn and explained to me, I still didn't understand, so my parents invited an overwhelmed Nick over for dinner one time. To make the night extraspecial, we even ordered pizza. I hadn't told Nick anything, but from the way he looked at me when I opened the door, I knew that my parents had explained to him what had happened. When they both finally explained what abortion meant, and I finally understood it, I was angry. Death? They want me to kill the baby before it was born?

I signed furiously. "I am not a murderer!" Aimee was staring at me from across the table, her hand surreptitiously over her belly. I hadn't directly spoken to Aimee privately since I found out she was pregnant. In many ways, I found relief in this. Aimee wasn't reaching out to talk to me, but she did stare at me a lot. We hadn't pulled out the notebook in a week, not since her last words were. "I am pregnant." And we both were inadvertently avoiding each other. The distraction from my parents was a relief.

Aimee had told a few friends and she mentioned that she let her sister know, but needed us to be with her when she told her mother. At first, Dad refused, signing to me while telling Aimee and my mom that it wouldn't help if we were there, and that her mother would respect her more if she was told her mother without us there. Mom disagreed immediately, saying that a Mother never wants to know if her daughter was a pregnant teen. Mom had also caught Aimee's scared eyes when Dad refused. I did too, I don't think I have ever seen anyone so terrified my entire life. And I love horror movies.

Aimee's mother brushed past us carrying her withered red purse and a box of cigarettes. She glared at me when she rushed out, and slammed the door as hard as she could. Mom had been standing in front of me the entire time, her back toward us so I could not see what she was saying to Aimee's mother. Aimee obviously heard what our mothers were saying, but I couldn't and for that I was very grateful. She turned around and signed. "Aimee's going to stay with us." She looked at Aimee, and smiled softly. "Get some clothes and everything you need. We'll come back later for anything else." She paused and with a sheepish smile. "Better get as much as you can though. Your mother is not too happy."

Aimee hadn't learned any proper sign language, but she tried to sign to me, but gesturing pointing upstairs and slowly saying. "Help me?" I looked at Mom if that was okay and Mom gave me a look of exasperation.

"Now you're worried about going up to Aimee's room?" she signed jokingly. Even Aimee had to grin.

When we got upstairs to her room, Mom waited downstairs, signing that she is going to wait downstairs and help herself to a cup of tea. Aimee showed her where the earl grey was and headed upstairs with me. I have noticed that Aimee and I hadn't really "talked" about what happened. We haven't talked about what we were going to do with the baby, if we were going to keep the baby, if we were going to give the baby up for adoption, or what . . .

Once in Aimee's room, I tapped Aimee' on the shoulder and mimed writing on my palm. Aimee nodded and handed me an old notebook that we had once used and then left. It was at the beginning of our dating. Sitting on the edge of her bed, I pulled a pen out of my jacket and wrote down. "I don't think you gave me enough paper to write what I have to say." I added a happy face to show I was just making light of things, and handed the notebook to Aimee who was dumping things out of her gym bag and school bag. Aimee took the notebook and grinned. "I don't think there are enough trees in the world to make enough paper to say what we have to say to each other." Aimee also added a happy face and a heart. I grinned and took a deep breath. Then I wrote, "How are you feeling?"

Aimee was throwing anything she can toss into her bag, including dumping out an entire drawer from her dresser and scooping the contents into the gym bag. She glanced at the notebook and looked at me straight in the eye. She shrugged. I cocked my head to the side and quickly jotted down. "You don't know how you feel?"

Aimee shrugged again without meeting my eyes and then looked down. I saw her shoulders heave, and I knew she was about to cry. I slid down to the ground beside her and wrapped my arms around her. Aimee seemed to have been holding her tears for some time because the minute I wrapped my arms around her, her body suddenly collapsed, and the tears were dry heaving tears. She was grabbing unto me, tightly, as if she was trying to make sure I wouldn't let go. I pressed my cheek against hers, and I suddenly was not sure whose tears were falling. Mine or hers.

I don't know how long I held Aimee like that, but it felt like a long time. I felt her body shaking as she guffawed her tears out, huge heaps of tears falling from her eyes. Her tears were contagious. It was a weird feeling, knowing that our communication was limited, yet we are both speaking through our tears. My chest was heaving at the same beat as Aimee's, as we both cried out the uncertainty of our future. As I was hugging Aimee, rocking her back and forth, letting my own misery combine with hers, I felt another pair of arms hug me from behind and wrap her arms around me and reaching past Aimee's back. I knew that hug so well, and it only made me cry even more, which made Mom hug us tighter. I felt the back of my T-shirt immediately soak as Mom's own tears fell from her eyes.

For some reason, having Mom hug me made me want to crawl into her arms and stay there forever. It felt good that the roles have changed, and I didn't have to protect Aimee anymore. I didn't want to be a father. What am I going to do? I couldn't be a father. Is the baby going to be deaf like me? How am I going to hear when the baby cries? Am I going to college? How will I afford a baby? Should I quit high school?

The only baby in my life who I have ever had a relationship with was my sister, Emma, whom I fell in love with the minute she grinned her bare-toothed smile at me. I will never forget the way I felt as an older brother. I knew my parents adopted me and took me in as their own child. This was something they never hid from me, mostly because of the fact that it is pretty obvious we are not blood related. I would eventually ask one day why I was caramel colored, Mom was chocolate colored, and Dad was vanilla with chocolate swirl colored.

Mom and Dad were very open about where they had adopted me, the culture differences between the three of us. It was very evident and a huge part of our lives, and this awareness always made me somewhat self-conscious of the fact that I was very different. We were not some after-school special kind of family where everything is very rosy. I always felt so different from my parents; because I know how much they love me, they always pointed out how different we were. It was evident in how they brought me up, how they raised me, how they spoke to me, and how most of their "life lessons" were sentences on the dry erase board where the sentences started with "Back in Ghana . . ." or "Back in Costa Rica . . ."

So when Emma was born, most of the attention was on her, and as she grew up she never made it obvious that we were different. She just knew we were brother and sister. Watching Emma grow up, I had my bouts of jealousy. Seeing her as my parents' child, their own flesh and blood, and knowing that I wasn't always felt like a clench in my heart. But all Emma had to do was smile at me and all of a sudden, I felt so much love in my heart.

I had binders and collections of Emma's drawings to me, and all her family drawings were with me holding her hand. Dad had framed the second one that Emma drew when she was three years old. Emma had drawn her very first family drawing of the four of us, where she had me holding her hand. We laughed when I saw she had drawn an "x" for my ears, as she had fully understood that I couldn't hear what is said.

I had kept that picture with me for four months straight, sleeping with the folded, tattered paper under my pillow, kept it in my pocket, took it with me to the bathroom, and it went out with me everywhere. I carried it in the front pocket of my favorite green sweater, and one evening Mom did the laundry and had forgotten to check the front pocket. When Mom found the miserable white pulp of paper splattered all around the washing machine, she took me aside and explained that she made a mistake. I was so angry that I didn't speak to her for a week. Mom tried to make it up with drawing the picture back for me as memory, as well as Dad and Emma, but I was attached to that particular picture. Dad framed Emma's second one, but I still thought about that drawing from time to time.

With Mom and Dad there, Emma always knew how to communicate to me. Emma learned simple sign language and had her own fair share of her moments on the dry erase board. Emma loved acting things out, but Mom and Dad always spoke to her while signing. How am I supposed to speak to my own kid? How am I supposed to do this without them? I knew that Mom and Dad would do their best to help me, as they explained to me as best as they could that they would support any decision I will ever make. Dad said that whatever Aimee decided to do, I should stand by her. Mom disagreed. "What if Simon wants to keep the baby?"

Dad threw his hands up in the air and then signed. "Then we will deal with it. But there are two people involved. Aimee and Simon need to talk about this together."

I shook my head miserably. "Aimee and I have not talked about this yet," I signed.

Mom nodded understandingly and signed, "You will. You both need to talk to each other. Right now, it is very scary." Aimee and I only had a chance to communicate to each other that night, as we finally packed up the rest of Aimee's stuff and headed home. Aimee didn't look back at her house, but we saw her mother sitting across the street in her own car, waiting for us to leave, cigarette smoke circulating around the room.

It took another week of Aimee living at our house, as Mom and Dad set up Emma's room as Aimee's room. Aimee protested, saying that Emma didn't and shouldn't have to give up her room for her, but Mom and Dad had a huge fight already on where Aimee would be staying. Mom thought it was completely inappropriate for us to share a room and we wouldn't fit anyways because I slept in a single bed. Dad thought that it was best that we learned to sleep together so we can "bond" as parents.

In the end, they both lost, as I gave up my room for Aimee and slept on the couch in the living room. Of course, that first night, we all had dinner together. Mom had gone out before dinner with Aimee and bought her prenatal vitamins and also some Chinese takeout. Dad protested when they came home, signing quickly that Chinese takeout wasn't healthy and Aimee needed to eat healthier now for her and the baby. Mom brushed his protests aside, signing that a pregnant woman needs to give in to her cravings and tonight was Aimee's first night at the house.

I noticed that the dry erase board was turned backward and pushed up against the wall. After dinner, Emma and I cleared the table, and Dad motioned for us to sit back at the dinner table. Mom scooped out bowls of ice cream, and Dad rolled out the dry erase board and flipped it over. In bold letters, Mom had written, "RULES FOR THE NEW PARENTS TO BE IN THIS HOUSE."

> Rule #1: No sex in the house.
> Rule #2: No sneaking to have sex anywhere in this house.
> Rule #3: No sneaking in the middle of the night to have sex
>   in this house.
> Rule #4: No sex at all until Aimee has her baby.
> Rule #5: This includes 96 and all forms of oral sex.

Mom had taken Emma and their bowls of ice cream into the living room to watch some TV while Dad slowly and confidently signed every single rule. He underlined "No" as he went through the list. I glanced at Aimee who looked like she was trying really hard to hold back laughter. She had pursed her lips in and her eyes were gleaming with mirth. Mom had snuck in during Dad's lecture and I glanced back to see Emma with her eyes glued to the TV and turned back to Dad's lecture, who kept his eyes glued to me.

Mom stood to the side, reading the list and looked at Dad with her eyes wide open. She marched over to the list and changed the 96 to a 69. Aimee all of a sudden fell off the chair, laughing so hard, and Dad looked confused. Mom glanced at me wearily and finally erased Rule #5 with her hand. As if in school, I raised my hand. Dad nodded at me.

I signed. "What is oral sex?" while Dad translated, turning red as he realized what he was translating.

Suddenly, I saw Aimee completely fall on the floor, holding her sides, laughing so hard that she couldn't breathe. That can't be good for the baby, but I wasn't quick enough to sign this. Mom started to laugh too, and so did Dad. Aimee, still laughing, went over to the dry erase board and drew a 6. Then a 9. And then happy faces in the 6 and 9. I laughed along with them. But I didn't admit that I still had no idea what that meant.

Aimee had a part-time job at a retail store and only worked Saturday and Sundays. I asked Jeff if I could work another day during the week, and he said it was fine, but Mom wasn't too happy about it.

"We can find a way to make it work, Simon, you need to focus on school."

I shook my head. "I am fine. School is easy."

I was lying. School was getting harder. All I could think of was Aimee. Aimee had made the huge decision to not complete college courses for a while, and just work full-time. She picked up a job at a market research company where she called people around North America and asked them to do surveys with her on the phone. She wrote about her first few days on the job on a notebook to me, and I was appalled at how rude some people can be. I signed this to Aimee, who smiled and shrugged, writing down that. "No one really likes to be bothered during dinner, but someone has to do it."

Some of her stories were funny: some lady had spent an hour with Aimee on the phone, but Aimee had a hard time hearing her because she had a really hard-to-understand accent (Aimee had to explain to me what "accent" was, and it took a whole page to explain it. I still don't know what "accent" means), so a survey that was only supposed to take ten minutes lasted an hour. Aimee shared the accounts of her new job with the family, and always had a written version for me to read during dinner.

Aimee and I had not really spoken about what we were going to do but we both knew that we were not going to have an abortion. Aimee said she refused to do it and would rather give up the baby up for adoption if anything. I too cannot have that on my conscience. But I was different from Aimee. I wouldn't be carrying the baby at all in my stomach, and the thought of a baby in her stomach kind of made me feel ill. I was afraid to ask stupid questions like. "Are you going to fall over?" with "Will it squash the baby?."

The one question that I feared the most was "Will the baby be deaf too?" It is hard to believe that there are other parents out there who would adopt a baby who is deaf too. My parents were special people and I love them to death. What if my baby turned out to not have the ability to hear as well? What if that baby had my nose, my hair, my Moroccan smile, and my deafness? These were things I could not tell anyone, not Aimee, not Nick, not my parents.

Especially not Aimee, who seemed to have fallen into her own little world ever since she moved in with us. She kept working to help pay for her stay at our house, but both my parents refused. Aimee felt terrible that she was living for free, so I asked Mom to just pretend to take the money, and Dad opened up a bank account for the baby under my name. I was also contributing to this baby, but not as much as Aimee as I was still in high school and Aimee was a little older than me. Aimee worked more hours, and she wrote once that the way people treated her at work on the phone was a perfect distraction to what was happening to her body.

One morning I heard Emma run to the living room where her mouth was moving frantically, but I couldn't read her lips, but she just grabbed my hand and tried her hardest to get me to come with her. I followed Emma upstairs to see Aimee kneeling on her knees in front of the toilet and Mom holding her hair up and rubbing her back beside her. Mom saw me but couldn't sign. With a free hand, she held up a finger as if to say "hold on," and I read her lips as she said to Emma, "Get Aimee a glass of water and one of your hair clips." Emma ran out of the washroom, pushing me out of the way, and I hit my back on the wall. I signed to Mom, "What's wrong? Is the baby dying?"

Mom looked confused with my question and then with a sudden realization signed, "Aimee is having morning sickness. It is normal when you are pregnant."

Aimee was sick for an entire month, She would be doing simply nothing and all of a sudden she would stand up and run to the washroom. The first few times I didn't want to go and see her vomit, but then after Dad pushed me into the bathroom once, I saw that I didn't have to watch, and I just do what Mom did that time, hold her hair up and rub her back. Aimee was usually done vomiting in five minutes.

"You need to try to encourage her to eat more," Dad signed to me, one evening when we were washing the dishes and I saw that Aimee barely touched her plantains and rice. (Mom cooked dinner that night, and she was convinced that boiled plantains and rice was the perfect way to nourish a baby in the belly. Emma and I made peanut butter and margarine sandwiches, and after dinner, Dad made one for himself too.)

The doctor for Aimee's OB something was a very nice woman named Dr. Channouf. She was older than Mom and wasn't shy about showing her gray hair. She had kind eyes and a very calm demeanor. I liked her immediately. We were supposed to meet her several times throughout the pregnancy. Dr. Channouf asked us what we were planning on doing since we were "having an unplanned child at an unplanned time." When my mom told her that I was deaf, she grinned at me. Then she turned to Mom and asked, "Completely?" Mom was furiously signing everything that was being said while Aimee was jotting down notes as quickly as a university student on steroids. Mom cocked her head from side to side and made this waving motion with her hand, as if to say, "Not really." Mom hated it when people asked if I was completely deaf.

Then Mom said, "Speak slowly. Simon can read lips. He can also read body language very well." She looked quite proud of this and looked over at me fondly. I grinned back and looked at Aimee, who was smiling at me. Then I saw Aimee look up to the doctor and say something. Mom immediately started to sign. "I am writing everything down for Simon too, so it would be really nice if you spoke slower as well for me." Dr. Channouf was more than willing, and she was very supportive of this. She wrote down on a piece of paper too. "You need to see me this time, three weeks from now, and then once a month."

I looked up at the doctor and nodded. Dr. Channouf lowered her chin and looked at me directly. "You need to be very supportive of Aimee throughout all of this. There are times when you may have another doctor. Dr. Mo is also very good, and she works with me too." I suddenly felt so guilty. I looked at Aimee, who smiled and reached over and grabbed my hand. I squeezed it tightly, as this was the first time we had held hands like this since the news of her baby. Mom was looking at me, nodding.

"What are you going to do with the baby?" Dr. Channouf signed. I could tell from her face that she was looking down on the fact that we were teenagers who were having babies. Aimee had mentioned that it bothered her, she felt that everyone was looking down at her. Aimee's grandmother had called Aimee in anger, had traced her back to our house telling Aimee that she was "disowned" and that she never wanted to see Aimee again. Aimee didn't even cry, although this was the same grandmother whom she spoke so lovingly about while growing up. It seemed that something inside Aimee had died, and it was nice to see her reach over and hold my hand again. I can read her body language so well, and although I knew deep down that she wasn't blaming me or accusing me of the pregnancy, I knew that she wasn't sure how to act around me anymore.

Things have changed. Things were going to keep changing. I loved Aimee, and she knew that. Aimee loved me too, and she told me that she wasn't leaving me at all. I knew too that she felt alone. She had written in a notebook, started a diary for the baby, and didn't tell me about it. I had found it one day when I was looking for a pair of my socks in my room and saw that although Aimee had fixed the bed nicely, she was a wonderful houseguest; she did not tuck the notebook away completely. I found this one Sunday morning when she was working and Jeff had closed the meat shop for a day because inspectors were coming. I didn't mean to open it and read, but I was surprised that Aimee had started writing in this journey for the baby (as she had started each diary entry as. "Dear Baby" before she even told me she was pregnant. I didn't know what to think about that, but it was a whole full week before she told me when she started on the diary entries.

I was also surprised to see that she wrote pages and pages of her fears, what she was going to do, how she felt, and how she didn't know what I will think when she tells me. I was going through my own fears and thoughts, and Aimee was going through her own, and it was then I realized how irresponsible it was for us to be parents at such a young age. I knew then that I was going to tell Aimee that night that I would prefer for the baby to be adopted. When Aimee came home, I came clean about how I had read her journal, and she wasn't even angry. She looked relieved and hugged me when I handed her a long letter I wrote. I didn't apologize for reading her diary, but I did say that I read it and was feeling the same way.

Aimee had mentioned in her diary that she was afraid that the baby will be deaf too. I had asked Aimee in the letter why didn't she tell me anything before and pulled out my own journal where I was writing down how afraid I was. I hadn't written in months since I met Aimee but started again when Aimee told me she was pregnant. Most of the words in my journal were completely choppy, and I felt shy about showing Aimee my journal. In the beginning I had blamed her for not knowing that we were supposed to use protection and I used my disability as an excuse. I signed this so to Nick one evening when we went out for pizza, just him and me.

"It doesn't matter if you are deaf, Simon. Your penis still works," Nick signed then picked up his beer bottle. He finished it off. I didn't move, as I was ashamed to realize that this was completely true.

Nick looked at me when he put the bottle down and signed, "Holy shit."

I signed and signed back, "I know."

"You being a father goes to show that it doesn't matter at all if you are deaf or not. You can't use that excuse anymore."

After that night I had found out Aimee was writing to the baby, we came to my parents and explained that we wanted to give the baby up for adoption. I signed this to my parents, and both my parents looked happy with the decision.

"Are you okay with this completely, Aimee?" I saw Mom sign to Aimee, who nodded furiously. She went over to the dry erase board and wrote, "I am only nineteen years old and Simon's only eighteen. Simon is adopted, and we can only hope that the baby will be adopted by parents like you both."

I grinned at my parents and felt such love for them. Dad looked at me and smiled, and came over and gave me a big bear hug.

"If you were thinking of keeping the baby, you know that Mom and I would be there for you and Aimee, right?"

Aimee and I both nodded.

"Are you sure you are going to be okay with giving up your child, though?" Mom signed to us both. She looked directly at Aimee and I suddenly realized why Mom was asking so persuasively.

I looked at Mom who glanced at me. "Giving up your baby is very hard."

I felt electricity all over the room, my body was tingling. I knew that my parents wanted to give up Emma at first because she has a mild form of Down syndrome. It was detected when Emma was still in the womb, and with all the upbringing they had with me and my adoption, it was easy to see that Mom was affected by the choice that we made.

Dad looked at Aimee and signed to me saying. "Do not do anything that will make us happy. Simon's mother and I will support anything you decide." Aimee nodded. No one communicated for a few moments. Then Mom looked at me. "Simon, are you very sure?"

I looked at Aimee and thought of how horrible the vomiting was. I nodded.

"Very sure," I sign-spelled. Deep down, though, I was lying. Seeing Mom's face, I realized, that there may be more than meets the eye.

Aimee and I kept the journal up though. We both decided to name the baby Quinn. It is a boy's name and also a girl's name, so that way we had covered all grounds. Aimee said that she always liked the name "Quinn" and I agreed it was a nice name. Simple too. We didn't tell my parents that we had the journal because I had a feeling Mom would be worried of the emotional attachment to the baby if we were writing to the baby in the journal. But Aimee wanted to keep the journal.

"It helps me get through the tough days," she wrote to me on a napkin when we were having lunch together one weekend. I nodded and wrote on the napkin. "That's why I write too. Too much going on in my head. Easier to write to figure things out."

Aimee looked at me for a second and then grabbed another napkin. She started to write on the napkin, as I sipped my Coke, I saw that scribbled what she started to write and then crumpled up the paper. She opened her bag and started rummaging in her bag, so I reached into my bag and pulled out my own notebook and slid it across the table.

Aimee saw the notebook and grinned and wrote, "How are you feeling, really, about everything?" I read the note upside down. I looked at Aimee and shrugged. I sign-spelled, "Scared," and Aimee nodded. Slowly, she sign-spelled, "Me too." I reached over and held her hand. It was shaking. Or was it mine?

I turned the paper over and took a deep breath before writing this. "I think I may want to keep the baby." I closed my eyes shut, something I did every time I wrote something down for my parents and was afraid to see what they their reaction will be. Emma had learned to do that as well, which was funny since she can still hear what is being said.

Aimee didn't tap me and the suspense was killing me so I finally opened one eye. And then the other. Aimee was staring at me as if she saw a ghost.

"What do you mean you want to keep the baby?"

I shrugged and wrote, "We haven't looked into adoption agencies yet, we are doing that next week." I was surprised at how calmly I was writing this. Was this selfish of me? Aimee was the one who was carrying the baby. How can I afford to keep the baby? Does my say matter? I wrote all these questions down, and Aimee started to cry. I handed her some napkins and wrote, "I am just asking. I don't know how I feel."

"But you have thought about us keeping the baby?" Aimee wrote. Before she can pass it to me, she wrote, "Why didn't you ever tell me how you really felt?" I sighed. I don't know why I never told her. Maybe because she's been crying every day and everything is happening so fast. But how do you say that to your crying, emotional girlfriend when you can't communicate in the first place? I shrugged. I didn't want to talk about it anymore. I wrote, "Can you please ask the waiter to bring me a Coke?"

Chapter 10

Aimee and I didn't speak that entire week. I went to school, hung out with Nick and only saw Aimee at home. I told Nick how I was feeling but the day was approaching when we would be having our appointment with an adoption agency. It was a terrible week, as I wrote down the pros and cons. I can do it, can't I? Aimee didn't have to be a part of my life or the baby's life if she didn't want to. She can just give birth and then I can take care of it, and if the baby needs to eat from her boobs, I can just go over . . .

Nick watched me sign all this frantically to him with a calm look on his face. When my hands stopped signing, Nick gave me a look. Then he signed. "Are you done?"

I shook my head miserably. "When did everything get so complicated?"

Nick signed. "When you didn't wear a condom." Even I had to laugh and threw the remaining chunks of ice from my cup on to Nick who laughed and tried to dodge them.

"Seriously though, Simon, I don't know what to say. You have to go to the adoption appointment tomorrow."

I nodded.

"When was the last time you and Aimee wrote to each other?"

I told him when I asked for the Coke a week ago. Nick made a funny face and signed.

"You guys live in the same house. How do you avoid communicating to each other?"

Easy. I just stopped writing to Aimee. But not to my journal. I wrote every single night, page and pages of how I was feeling. As an adopted child, I know that I was blessed to have such great parents. They were very supportive of me, and I loved them so much. As much as I loved my family though, I felt . . . I don't know. I see Aimee's tummy, and there is now a noticeable bump. I never touched it, and Aimee never asked me to. But I noticed that she kept her hand on it all the time too. Sometimes just rubbing her belly. I tried to picture sometimes what the baby looked like. I assumed that the baby would look exactly like me. With Dad's Costa Rican nose and Mom's fuzzy hair. Emma's dimples and personality. I knew that the baby wouldn't look anything like them, but it was nice to imagine so.

When I wasn't feeling anger toward Aimee or resentment, I liked to think that the baby had her eyes and smile. Giving up this baby means that there is someone out there, who will actually have my blood and my looks, and I won't even get to be with the baby. I think that is what was hurting me inside. I had my family, my wonderful mom, my supportive and amazing dad, and my incredible sister. Those three people meant the whole world to me, but I didn't look anything like them. How could I do that? How can I just have that thought that someone out there, who really has my genes, my blood, my deafness, is out there and I give him up?

Maybe it would have been easier, I don't know, if I wasn't adopted and I actually did belong to my parents. I thought back to my biological parents and wondered if they ever thought about me. Thinking about being a father made me think about my Moroccan parents all the time, if they even thought about me, if they even cared that I existed. I didn't want my baby to feel like that. No one ever reached out to me, no Moroccan couple had ever shown up at my door and asked if I was their child and if they want to have a relationship with me. No one ever sent me a postcard from Morocco asking me if I was their son. No one in Morocco seemed to care that I was deaf. How can I just pass this thought to my own son or daughter?

Aimee didn't understand, she looked like her mother. I was convinced that once the baby was born, her mother would find a way to be close to her again. She would reach out for Aimee. No one ever reached out to me. I loved my parents, but they didn't look like me. I always felt disconnected from them somehow because it was so obvious that we were not related. I knew they loved me. I don't know what to think.

"You have to figure out what you want to do by tomorrow. You need to discuss how you are feeling to Aimee. If you need me there, I will. But this is your child as much as hers," Nick signed. He continued. "You have been silent for so long, you can't just let this go by. If you feel you want to take care of the baby, you need to talk to Aimee about it. You know that your parents will be there to support you, you know that I will be here to support you and you know that Aimee will at least reconsider what you are thinking. No one knows how you feel. You are an adult now, and making huge changes in your life. There is another person involved now, and just because you can't see this other person, you know that this person exists. You need to think clearly. You have to figure out if you are being selfish or not."

He let his hands rest for a bit and looked at me. I held my breath for what felt like a lifetime. Then finally, I signed back. "I want to keep the baby."

I came home and waited for Aimee to come home while I played a card game with Emma. I already told my parents what I wanted to do, and they were very supportive.

Once I explained how much it meant to me to have someone out there who looked like me, who was a part of me, they completely understood. I saw that Mom wanted to protest at first, but I signed so fast, in front of the dry erase board, with the marker opened and ready in case I needed to explain something specific. They both understood immediately.

I signed before they can ask. "One day, I will go to college. But right now, I want to raise this baby." Mom, Dad, and Emma left the house for the evening to go to some errands and shopping so Aimee and I can have some privacy. Dad made a gesture to text him on his cell phone if I needed him immediately and I nodded. When Aimee came home, I had everything ready. My explanations were on paper, on the dry erase board and all my Plan Bs. I didn't have a Plan B when I explained everything to my parents, but Mom suggested that I do have one for Aimee because she may not be so agreeable.

When Aimee came through the door, she was surprised to see me sitting on the staircase near the door, so I would be the first person she would see. I gave her a half-smile and waved, and Aimee smiled back softly. She waved. I stood up and walked slowly over to her, scared to see if she will hit me when I walk over to her. We hadn't exchanged any notes to each other for a whole week. Nothing at all. We avoided each other's eyes and everyone in the house knew we were not on "communicating terms."

My parents did not interfere at all. I think they wanted to see if we could sort this out ourselves. If Aimee wasn't pregnant with my child, for sure they would be all over us like white on rice. But having a baby has a funny way of all of a sudden turning people into adults.

Aimee didn't move when I approached her, but I all of a sudden saw the belly and my heart was filled with an overwhelming feeling of love. Suddenly, Aimee walked over to me and held her arms out. The minute I saw that she did, I dove immediately into her arms. She wrapped her arms around my head and I felt the belly between us. I held her tightly and once again, our tears flowed into one river.

I didn't even have to explain anything to Aimee. She wanted to keep the baby too. As I was crying into her shoulders, she held my head back When Mom, Dad and Emma came home, we were still hugging in the hallway. I couldn't stop crying. I was happy but *wow*, I am going to be a father! Aimee and I are going to raise a baby together! My parents were happy with whatever decision we made and everything fell into a huge group hug. I saw Aimee kneel in front of Emma and tell her that she was going to be an aunt. Emma squealed. Emma understood that Aimee was going to have a baby and that I was the father, but she also knew that we had originally planned to not keep the baby. Seeing how happy Aimee seemed and feeling the happiness in my heart, I knew that we made the right decision.

Mom called the adoption agency the next day to let them know that we were not going to come in for an appointment. Aimee kept smiling all day, and it suddenly occurred to me that Aimee may have wanted to keep the baby the whole time, but was afraid of what to think and what to do. She had written to me that she and Rachel had met up and Rachel had told her to follow her heart.

Chapter 11

I met my mom and Aimee at the coffee shop across the doctor's. The crisp fall weather hit us, but I felt warm all over. On cloud nine. They were in midtalk when I approached. Their lips were moving too fast, I couldn't catch what they were saying. The looks on their faces though was all smiles. Both Aimee and Mom grinned when they saw me. Mom was wearing a long warm gray coat that was not buttoned and had a red scarf wrapped around her head. Aimee was wearing jeans, sneakers, and an oversized white sweater. She had her hair wrapped up in a messy bun that made her look absolutely beautiful. I lightly touched her belly to say hello. I leaned forward to kiss Mom on the cheek, then followed by giving Aimee a kiss on her cheek. Shyly. Mom noticed my face and rolled her eyes. "No need to be shy now" she signed. Aimee laughed.

"We have an hour before the appointment and the secretary already knows we're here" Aimee said, looking at me while Mom interpreted. I nodded. Aimee made an eating motion. "Hungry?"

"Starving." I imitated her gesture with an exaggerated nod. I made the sign for a cup of coffee. Then "Please." One of the few signs Aimee learned from dating me.

"Coffee? Since when did you drink coffee?" Mom signed, giving me a startled look.

"It's a grown-up drink," I signed, making my cutest I'm-still-your-baby-boy face. Mom interpreted to Aimee, giving me a weary look. Aimee threw her head back and laughed, then started to walk across to the coffee shop. I fell into step with Mom, who tapped me on the arm and signed. "You could have just done with the coffee, not the baby."

Aimee seemed nervous when we arrived in the waiting room. She kept squeezing my hand as if it was a stress ball. Having had a small cup of hot chocolate, she thanked Mom profusely for being able to be at the appointment. She apologized for her parents not being able to come, and that they were still not ready to admit she was pregnant. Mom was doing her best to sign and interpret, but I knew she was downplaying what Aimee was saying. We held hands, and the nurse called us into the room. Aimee changed behind a closed curtain and the doctor greeted us when we were ready. I felt nervous. I hadn't met this doctor. Mom and Aimee had. Aimee's sister had accompanied her to the doctor as well and knew this doctor. I saw Aimee's lips move and the doctor smiled at me, extending her hand, her lips moving. I was so nervous that I didn't get what she said. I suddenly felt tears in my eyes and blinked quickly to hide them.

Mom hurriedly explained during the introduction that I was deaf. Dr. Mo pursed her lips and then smiled. She took out a sheet of blank paper and wrote, "My name is Dr. Mohamed. Please call me Dr. Mo." I finished reading before she turned it over to me. I had perfected reading upside-down when I was four. I nodded and shook her hand. Mom signed. "He's the father." Dr. Mo didn't acknowledge this. She sat down and gestured for all three of us to do the same. I wrote on the paper. "Where is Dr. Channouf?"

Dr. Mo smiled. "She is on vacation with her daughter in Turkey. They will be there for a few weeks as Dr. Channouf's daughter Ivana is getting married." She smiled as Mom signed this. Then she went back to business.

"Who are you in relation to Simon?" Dr. Mo asked Mom.

Mom quickly interpreted to me and I held up my hand. I didn't want to be excluded. I grabbed her pen. "She's my mom."

Dr. Mo's face didn't change. Aimee pressed her knee into mine. I pressed back, my heart beating. Mom nodded quickly. "Simon's my son. We adopted him."

Dr. Mo smiled. I couldn't read her smile. It seemed fake. Aimee started talking and I got lost. Mom couldn't interpret fast enough for me, so we both sat back and let Aimee talk. Dr. Mo and Aimee spoke. I didn't bother to try to read their lips. My shoulders were hunched up. This was harder than I thought. Mom looked like she was watching a tennis match. She didn't even bother to try to sign what they were saying. What were they saying? Was Dr. Mo surprised that I was adopted? That I was deaf and mute? That I'm only eighteen years old and Aimee's only seventeen? (and a half). That we were planning on keeping our baby?

After a few minutes, Dr. Mo pushed her chair back. Aimee stood too. Aimee said a few words to Mom and reached down to squeeze my shoulder. I looked expectantly up at Mom.

"Check up, Simon. Want to see your baby?" Mom asked. All of a sudden, I didn't want to. I shook my head. Dr. Mo looked at me and smiled. She raised her hand up as if to say "It's okay." I read her mouth. "You don't have to." I looked up at Aimee, who looked hurt. "You don't want to see your baby?" she asked. She didn't bother to try to sign. I knew what she said. I wanted to say sorry, yes I do. But I would be lying. Mom signed. "It's just a checkup, Sai. Just to see how the baby is doing." I shook my head again. I kept shaking. I started to count how many times I was shaking my head when Aimee abruptly stopped me. I didn't look up. Aimee and Mom walked away. Dr. Mo glanced at me before they left the room. I hated the look on her face. A look of disapproval. A look of pity. She didn't even try to hide it.

Aimee had left her purse on the chair she was sitting on and I peeked in. I wanted to see if the journal was there. It was. I pulled it out gingerly and picked up the Dr. Mo's pen. Aimee had been the last one to write in the journal. I had come to depend deeply on the journal. I wrote more than Aimee did. Aimee's entries were short. Sometimes she expressed her anger at her family for not being supportive. Other times she wrote about how wonderful it would be to be a mother. The last journal entry was just a few hours ago.

"Hi, baby, it's too early to feel you kick, but I dreamt last night that you tried to. You were trying to say hello to me. I said hi back. I hope you're doing well in there, I have completely given up chocolate as it know makes me want to vomit, but your dad and I will make it up when you're old enough to go trick-or-treating. I tried to eat a salad today, for you, but ended up having a bag of chips to go with it. I brought a salad with tons of spinach. Some acid-vitamin-thing is very good for you, but it tasted disgusting. I'll try again tomorrow. Your dad and grandma (your good grandma) are coming with me to the check up later after school. I can't wait to teach you sign language. You're going to have to learn to communicate with your dad. I still have to learn. He's very excited to meet you. So am I. Seven more months to go. We can make it, baby. Love, Mommy."

Without realizing it, tears were flowing down my face. Oh my goodness, what kind of father am I going to be? Fathers don't cry! Well, mine does, but in general, *fathers don't cry*! The ones on television don't! My shoulders were shaking, and so was the pen in my hand. With my left hand, I tried to stop the pen from shaking. In cursive, because it looked mature, I wrote, "Seven more months to go, baby. Can't wait to see you. Love, Dad." My breath caught in my throat. "Love, Dad." For the first time ever, those words stood out. Jumped at me from the paper. I wrote it again. "Love, Dad." Again. And again. It kept jumping out at me.

I quickly shut The Journal to keep the words inside. I took a deep breath and glanced at the clock. They've been gone for a while. I didn't know which room they went, but I wanted to see the baby. I left the book on the chair and tried to see where they went. Suddenly a door opened, and they walked out. Aimee was zipping up her sweater and looked at me in surprise. Then she smiled, relieved I was trying to find them. So did Mom. Mom squeezed my arm in reassurance. Dr. Mo gestured back into the room with desk.

"Everything okay?" I signed to Mom. Mom signed back to Dr. Mo. Dr. Mo sighed. She fiddled around with the mouse on her laptop and looked through Aimee's file. She took the piece of paper in which she had introduced herself. She jotted down a few sentences. When she was down, she slowly turned it around to face us.

"According to your last week appointment with the prenatal test and blood work, there is a slight problem with your baby."

Mom turned her ear to one side, something she often does when she doesn't understand something. "What do you mean?"

Aimee leaned forward and I saw her lips move from the side, and the tears falling from her eyes. I can tell she was asking if the baby was deaf because Dr. Mo shook her head and said, "No, we can't determine that until the baby is born." Mom translated for me.

"What is it then?" Mom was translating what Aimee was saying as she noticed I was getting frustrated.

"Your baby has a birth defect."

Mom was quick. "What kind of birth defect?" she said, and then realized that she forgot to sign, and then signed for me. This didn't mean anything to me. What kind of birth defect? What is a birth defect? The doctor continued talking to Aimee and Mom signed silently to me. "Something is wrong with the baby. Like Emma."

Oh.

Ohhh.

I turned to Mom. "Exactly like Emma or like me?"

Mom shrugged and tried to get back into the conversation with Aimee and the doctor, putting her hand on my forearm to "shut" me up. I sat and stared at the floor.

Something is wrong with the baby.

The baby may have a disability like Emma. The baby may have Down syndrome. Or the baby may be deaf. Like me. Like me.

The baby may be deaf like me.

I started to feel dizzy. I put my head between my knees and shut my eyes really tight. I felt a hand on my back and from familiarity I knew it was Aimee's hand. It rubbed my back and then I raised my head. The doctor had left the room and Mom and Aimee were talking. Aimee wasn't upset nor was she crying. She looked remarkably calm and so did Mom. Maybe it was a mistake? I signed so to Mom who shook her head and simply signed. "No, it is not."

Aimee signed to me slowly. "Are you okay?"

I looked at Aimee and signed back. "Are you?" Aimee nodded.

I looked from Mom to Aimee and asked. "What is wrong with the baby? Is the baby deaf?" Mom signed to me. "We can't tell if the baby is deaf until the baby is born. The doctor says that the MRI test shows that the baby is missing some chromosomes, quite possibly be Down syndrome, although they can't tell yet."

"Is there medicine that the baby can take?" I signed to Mom, who interpreted for Aimee. Aimee shook her head. "You can't cure a birth defect," she wrote on the notebook and showed it to me.

"Did we do something wrong? Did Aimee not eat the right foods?" I signed to Mom. Mom interpreted and shook her head at me. "It may be genetic."

Okay. So maybe because Emma has it? I signed so to Mom, and Mom gave me a look.

Oh right. Emma isn't my blood sister. I'm adopted.

I'm adopted.

Oh my goodness. It might be because of my biological parents. I signed this to Mom with a look of triumph. Mom looked down sadly. "Maybe." I looked at Aimee who seemed calm. She had her hand on her belly and was rubbing it. I too reached over and rubbed the baby. Aimee put her hand on top of mine and smiled slightly. Mom hugged me and squeezed Aimee's shoulders.

"We will get through this for sure," she signed. The doctor came back in and spoke to Mom and Aimee for a few more minutes, but I signed to

Mom that I was going to use the washroom and excused myself quietly. I was dizzy. I felt lightheaded, and all the colors in the washroom were all of a sudden in my face. I shook my head quickly, back and forth, the way I see dogs do right after they take a bath. I kept shaking my head, trying to stop all the colors in the room from spinning around and around.

My baby has a disability. I didn't know what to do or think about that. I thought about Emma, with her button nose and her eyes too far apart, but with a smile that can melt the coldest of hearts. Will my baby be as beautiful as my sister? Mom and Dad had gotten support, I remember, when Emma was born. They met with a social worker as well once a month—who came to see Emma—and had also gotten counseling. His name was Robert. A Canadian from the city of Toronto. I remember because he had a gait in his walk and had a very friendly face. I didn't know men can be social workers. I remember that Dad put up a stink because there were no social workers who were skilled in Down syndrome and disabilities who can also sign, because my dad signed furiously. "My son needs to know everything about his sister too!" After that, a social worker, Zico from the Caribbean, short guy with glasses and an open personality, was found who could speak sign language but was not that skilled in disabilities, so both social workers came in to interpret for me. I remember being very impressed with both male social workers. The only social workers I have really met in the past were women social workers.

We worked with them for about three years, once a month. They watched as we spent time with Emma. Mostly individually for me. I didn't mind spending time with Emma with Zico and Robert watching. They didn't stand off to the side and made us feel like we were in a fishbowl; they spent time with us too. They colored, they drew, they made sand castles, they went down the slides and pushed me in the swings. I was really sad when Zico and Robert stopped working with us. I don't know what really happened. When I asked Mom a year later, she said that they both got married. Zico married a beautiful doctor in New Mexico and Robert met the love of his life in the other side of Canada.

Is that what I am going to have now for our baby? I sat on the toilet seat and tried to regain my breathing. Part of me now wished we had given up the baby for adoption, but the minute I thought about it, I felt such guilt. I felt my chest hurt. But what am I going to do? How are we going to raise a child when we are already so young? Now a baby with a disability? I remember how stressed Mom used to be. They were more overprotective of Emma. Not that they weren't overprotective of me, but I remember how much *more* overprotective they were over her. Will the baby be a boy? Or a girl?

Suddenly I started shaking. This was my fault. I am the reason why the baby has a disability. It must be. There is something in my genes. I remember the first time I head of the word "genes," and I looked down on what I was wearing that day, and Dad shook his head. "No, Simon." I thought back to my biological parents. I used to think of them as some king or queen in some far-off city in Morocco (especially when I was mad at my parents), but now I saw them as horrible, grotesque people who didn't care about me. They saw me with a disability and dropped me off in some Moroccan orphanage and didn't care what happened to me, because I wasn't "perfect."

I stomped my foot on the porcelain floor in defiance. *No!* I am not going to do that to my . . . suddenly, I saw the gap between the floor and the bathroom door: something moving. It was a finger! Oh! I stood up from the toilet seat and knocked my fist on the door, watching as the finger, a dark brown one, so Mom's, moved away from the door. I didn't realize how long I was in the washroom for, and I had locked it. When I opened the door, Aimee and Mom were standing there with the secretary, who was holding a key just in case. Mom looked relieved and Aimee was staring at me bug eyed.

"You were in the washroom for over an hour," Mom signed, gathering me in her arms. It felt so good to be in her arms. I hugged her with one arm and touched my pockets for my cell phone and saw that Aimee was carrying it. I left it. Aimee walked over to us, and Mom hugged her too. Then Mom pulled back and held me at arm's length and signed, while looking directly into my eyes, "Everything is going to be okay." I nodded. She looked at me strictly to make sure I understood her and signed again, "Simon, everything is going to be okay." She glanced at Aimee who was nodding encouragingly.

Chapter 12

Aimee and I kept up the journal. Aimee wrote in it more as I had fallen back on some assignments at school, and my high school called my parents saying that I was failing Math, Science, and Phys. Ed.

"Gym?" Nick signed incredulously to me when I told him at work. I nodded, my face red. "Gym."

Nick laughed and signed. "You may have flunked Sex Ed. too because they teach you to wear a condom." I laughed and threw pieces of ground beef on his white meat jacket that we are supposed to wear. Nick made a face and threw some ground pork at me, and I picked up a steak and winded up my arm to throw it at him . . . and it hit Jeff in the face. Nick was trying so hard not to laugh, and I turned around to see Jeff with a big steak on his face. The image was so funny, as he stood there, the steak meat bigger than his face. Jeff didn't even move, didn't even bother to take off the steak. I saw Nick grab his cell phone and quickly take a picture with his camera, still laughing. I couldn't laugh, I felt so bad. Jeff then peeled the steak off slowly off his face, and I instinctively took a few steps back.

Jeff kept his eyes closed, but his face was moist from the meat but I can see from his expression that he wasn't angry at all. I saw Nick leaning over the butcher counter, trying to catch his breath from laughing so hard. While looking at Nick, all of a sudden, I saw from the other corner of my eye Jeff wind back and whack the steak that was just on his face unto mine. It hurt.

Aimee got bigger and bigger. Since the baby had a birth defect, we had to go in more. Aimee was given a special diet that contained "Folic acid," which meant that Mom somehow made spinach every night. Spinach lasagna, spinach quiche, spinach salad. Emma made a face every single night when dinner was served that after a week Mom finally started just making her a sandwich. Aimee had to also drink vitamins and after dinner, the five of us went for a long walk.

Dad took me aside one evening when we were going for our evening walk, and signed that he was planning a weekend trip for us, just me and him.

"Weekend trip?" I signed, excitedly. But wait. "I can't leave Aimee!"

Dad signed, nodding his chin toward Mom, Aimee and Emma who had walked ahead of us, arms linked that. "I already spoke to them about it. We are just going away for two days. Camping and hiking up north."

"Without Mom and Emma too?" I signed.

"Yes, just the two of us."

We left that following weekend north of where we lived. It was only three hours away, and it was a campsite that had a lot of hiking. Dad was a little nervous, you can see, as we have never done such a trip before.

"Simon, you can't leave me. You need to be with me at all times. Our cell phones do not have reception here. I can't call you if you get lost." I nodded. But Dad seemed worried all weekend.

"Maybe we should do something else," Dad signed on our bus ride up there.

"Why?"

"Because, this could be a dangerous trip. I don't think I thought this through."

I was disappointed. Ever since Dad had mentioned this trip to me, I had gotten excited about it and asked Aimee if I could have the journal for the baby all weekend so I can write about my trip to the baby. "I won't leave you, I promise," I signed.

"But you can't wake up in the middle of the night and go wandering all over the place. You even have to wake me up if you want to go and pee," Dad signed sternly. Dad knew I always went to the bathroom in the middle of the night.

"It's only two days, Dad."

"But if you get lost, you won't be able to hear us call you. We can't use our cell phones here either." Dad looked miserable. "I'm an idiot. I didn't think things through."

"Well, I didn't get lost yet, so stop thinking I will."

"But what if you do?"

"What if I don't?" I squeezed Dad's arm. "I'm going to be a dad, Dad. Relax. I am not a kid anymore." Dad's face relaxed.

"But we still need to take extra precautions," Dad signed. "I've read crazy stories about people who get lost in the woods . . . but Mom thought it would be a good idea for us to talk about some things."

"What things?"

Dad smiled at me. "You're going to be a Daddy," he signed. "That's one of the most wonderful things in the world. I am so happy and lucky to have you and Emma."

I smiled back. "Is it hard? Being a Dad?"

Dad nodded immediately. "Very." He readjusted the way he was sitting and signed. "Your entire life changes. Everything is about your child. You think about them first before anything and anyone. Especially yourself."

I nodded.

"When you are sleeping at night and the baby wakes up, you need to be awake too. We will figure out everything once the baby is born, as we need you to have the lights flick on and off when the baby cries. Anyways, we will do our best to figure out how everything will happen. The baby will be awake all the time, ready to eat, you need to be there with Aimee. Also, we need to figure out what you are going to do about school. Do you want to take some time off for now? There are ways around where you can finish high school later on."

I nodded.

"I am still learning. Mom is still learning. Every day we are learning how to be parents. You are going to be parents for the rest of your life. So every day is a learning process," Dad signed. I nodded. "Mom and I will be there for you, Simon. Never forget that. We will never leave you alone in this. But this isn't all on us. You are the father. You need to take care of your child."

I nodded. Dad looked at me skeptically.

"Don't be afraid to jump in. I know it's a little harder that the baby has a birth defect that we are not sure of, but I'll tell you something, Simon. Mom and I are very happy to you have you and Emma. When Emma was born, it was stressful, but I never regretted having her. We never regretted adopting you. We knew you had a disability, and we still loved you from the start. This baby is a gift. You are very lucky to have this baby."

That weekend, as Dad and I set up the campsite, we saw that there were several families on a camping trip and Dad made it known that I was deaf. I didn't mind; Dad had never taken me on such a trip before and you can tell he was nervous. I spent every minute with my dad as he signed over and over and over stories of how he raised me and Emma, and how terrified he was the first time he had to change Emma's diapers, and how hurt he was when he and I had our first fight.

Dad and I have never spoken this much before, and I really appreciated it. Dad admitted that there were days when he didn't know what to do, and the only thing that pulled him through was his love for Emma and I. "And that is the most important thing. Love," Dad signed.

I smiled at him. "I am so lucky to have you and Mom," I signed. "I don't think there are parents out there like you, and that is another reason why I didn't want to give the baby up."

We hiked, and to appease Dad's stress, I tied a hiking rope around us so we were always tied together. Dad didn't seem to think of that and looked relieved when he saw that there was absolutely no way I would get lost, and that if I did, he would be lost with me.

"Mom and I don't have much money, but we do have some saved up and we are going to fix the basement up so you and Aimee have more room and the nursery will be there too," Dad signed when we were making s'mores. I licked my fingers as the strings of marshmallows dripped off the side of my graham cracker.

We talked about everything that weekend, what my plans were after the baby, how to finish school, and what I wanted to do in the future. I had no idea, but I mentioned to Dad that I wanted to be a writer and publish books, and maybe go to college and look into that.

"That is incredible Simon!" Dad signed, beaming at me. "I would love to read some of the things you wrote." So I shared Dad the journal that Aimee and I had for the baby and saw Dad read every single page slowly.

"This is absolutely beautiful Simon," Dad signed to me, his eyes tearing up. He reached over and hugged me. "I am very proud of you."

Chapter 13

When Aimee was seven months, her tiny frame had made her look bigger than when she was seven months. Dr. Mo had given us an option of surgery for the baby's defect, but Aimee was against it. "As far as I am concerned, this baby is perfect," Aimee said. Mom had signed this and I saw her face glow with love for Aimee. "There is no surgery needed."

Aimee and I, our relationship had faltered during the pregnancy. I had not had sex with her since we found out she was pregnant and she didn't seem interested in having sex with me either. It was weird to see the baby in her, but even though we were not being intimate, Aimee had grown more beautiful. She didn't seem like the Aimee I had fallen for, she seemed now like someone unattainable and I admired her from afar. Her hair glowed more, her eyes were brighter and she seemed to be glowing from inside. I felt a bit intimidated by her, as she seemed to be handling the pregnancy so well. The only thing we both shared was the journal for the baby.

"Have you tried contacting your mother?" Mom signed once one evening to Aimee and me.

Aimee nodded. "I called her and when she heard my voice she hung up." Aimee didn't seem sad about it, though, she just said it matter-of-factly. "I called my sister, and she asked me how I was doing and just to ignore Mom."

"Is this an older sister?" Mom signed.

"Kind of, she's my dad's half-daughter. We are not too close, but she's only three months older than me. It's kind of a long story. She and Mom do not get along." Aimee waved her hand away. "They are the only two families I have. Rachel knows my cousin, but we haven't spoken in years. I don't really have much of a family. You're the only family I have."

That weekend, Aimee called Mom, who called me at the butcher's shop to let Nick know that Aimee's water had broken prematurely. Nick signed this to me and I froze.

"That means the baby is ready to come, Simon," Nick signed quickly and then dialed the phone and Nick signed to me. "Jeff." I saw Nick speak quickly on the phone to Jeff and then Nick called a taxi.

"Jeff is on his way to watch the shop and we are going to the hospital," Nick signed. We had a new staff in the store, a quiet college man named Ivan, who was working the counter. Nick turned his back to me while telling him that what was happening and Ivan, who had only been at the store for a week and just met me earlier that week gave me a thumbs-up sign and grinned.

When Jeff arrived, Jeff shook my hand and got a taxi for Nick and me. Nick kept grinning at me on the ride there. "Wow."

I grinned back, but I was nervous. "Isn't it a little too early? We still have two more months to go. We still have eight weeks to go." My heart was thumping in my chest. I felt like it was going to burst of out of my chest. I was clutching my notebook with me, not the one for the baby, but one that I kept hidden from Aimee as I figured all this out on my own. Aimee had seen me with it, but she saw how I had tried to hide it from her, and she respected this and never pressed me to know what it was about.

Aimee, Mom and Emma were in the Triage room, just where the baby is about to be delivered. I ran to Aimee when I saw her, she was on the bed, and her face was pale. Emma waved at me and Mom signed. "Aimee has a bit of a fever." Nick took Emma's hand and led her out of the room, so Mom could be with us. Aimee held my hand and smiled at me. "I think it's time!" I read her lips and learned forward to hug her. I suddenly felt such love toward her, as she looked so frail in the bed. She looked like she was in pain. She turned and asked the nurse for a pencil and a pad of paper and the nurse handed her one from her pocket, smiling at me. Aimee wrote, "It's okay if you wait outside. As long as your Mom is here, I'm okay."

I think she wanted Mom's full attention instead of her signing back and forth to me. This stung, but I understood. Mom looked at me and I signed. "I'm going to wait outside with Nick and Emma. Is Dad coming?" Mom nodded and signed. "He'll be here as soon as work is done."

Nick looked up from the straw people he was making with Emma when I came out of the triage room and raised an eyebrow.

"Aimee has a fever and she asked that I wait out here," I signed. I couldn't keep the pain off of my face. At that moment, Rachel came through the elevator and waved at us coming over. She kissed Nick and gave me a hug and Emma a hug. Nick spoke, signing that Aimee had a fever. Rachel looked worried and went to the room where I pointed out.

"How is she doing?" Nick signed to me. He didn't speak as he didn't want to alarm Emma. Emma was playing with the straw that Nick had twisted into stick figures.

"She has a fever. She said it was best if I stayed out here. As long as my mom was there . . . ," I signed, trailing off. I felt something was wrong. Aimee always wanted me with her. Yes, our relationship wasn't the way it used to be, but Aimee had talked about how wonderful it would be when they announced if we had a baby girl or a baby boy.

I signed this to Nick, who signed back. "They are not delivering yet, so it's okay. If they were, they would be in the delivery room."

I couldn't keep the worried look off of my face. "Do you think she is okay? Is it going to hurt? She has a fever and she was really white."

Nick's expression changed when I mentioned this and he signed. "Don't worry." But you can tell that he was worried himself.

Dad arrived two hours later, and we were still sitting in the waiting room outside the triage. He was carrying bags of sandwiches from a nearby deli and when he saw me and Emma, he came over to us. Emma jumped up on him and he kissed Emma and hugged me. He too looked worried, and I knew that he had called Mom or Mom had called him to explain what happened.

I felt a chill in my heart. Mom had not once come out of the triage and neither did Rachel. I kept my eyes glued to the door. Nick had left with Emma for a bit and taken her down to the cafeteria to get her something to eat, but I didn't do anything but sit there and kept my eyes glued. I thought back to my journal, but I couldn't bring myself to write. Aimee's white face kept coming up.

Finally, Mom came out and she looked so stressed and worried but her kept a smile on her face. "We are going to the delivery room in half an hour," she signed to us.

"Is she okay?" I signed, standing up and trying to go right in front of her face so Dad wouldn't talk before me. Mom looked weary. "Aimee's got a high fever and she was hemorrhaging. She was bleeding inside," Mom signed slowly. Mom looked pained when she said the next words to me. "Aimee thinks it's best if you guys went home tonight. You can come back tomorrow morning." You can tell that she didn't agree with this but was just carrying out Aimee's request.

I was shocked. "She doesn't want me here?" I signed angrily.

Mom sighed and signed. "She's in a lot of pain, Si. A *lot*. She lost so much blood that we had to get a blood transfusion for her. It's best if you just went home and got some rest. The baby will be here soon. The baby is okay." Mom handed me a piece of paper. "This is Aimee's sister's number. When you get a chance, call her. I think her name is Caity."

I was shaking inside. "I don't want to go home! I want to be here!" I signed angrily. I stomped my foot, and Dad put a hand on my shoulder to calm me down. Nick was watching the entire conversation and you can see that there was more they were not telling me. *"What is going on? Why doesn't Aimee want me there?"* I signed furiously.

Mom looked like she was about to cry. "Please, Simon. She asked you to go home." With that, I started to cry. Nick stood up and led me toward the elevators. Rachel came out a few minutes later while Mom and Dad talked out of earshot. Dad turned his back and blocked me completely. Sudden rage exploded in me and I ran as quickly as I could to Aimee's room. I saw Dad trying to run after me, but Mom stopped him. I burst into Aimee's room and saw that she was asleep. I went over to her, angry and shook her awake. She stirred and a nurse came into the room, and then Nick. The nurse looked like she was trying to get me to leave, but I didn't care. I shook Aimee again, who looked so frail and white. She opened her eyes slightly and I just gave her the maddest look I could give. I couldn't even talk to her, she looked like trying to open her eyes was the hardest thing in the world. I put my hand on her stomach and she placed her hand on top of mine and rubbed my hand. Then she shook her head and opened her lips to say something to Nick. Nick nodded and leaned forward to kiss her on her forehead.

"Come, Simon. She's tired. They're going to let her rest before her contractions come again. The baby will be born soon, they are going to send her to the delivery room in an hour."

I signed. "Can you ask her to let me stay?" Aimee watched this and realized what I was trying to ask and pulled on my hand. I looked at her, but couldn't see from all the tears that suddenly was blocking us both. I saw her ask Nick something and Nick quickly dove to get her a piece of paper and a pen from her purse on the bedside table. The hand that was hooked to all the tubes reached for the pen and she wrote something on the piece of paper. She wrote slowly; it looked like she was having a hard time writing. Then she folded it and asked Nick something, but I read her lips. "Tell Simon to read it after the baby is born." I felt my anger slide off my body. I felt defeated.

Nick handed me the folded piece of paper and signed. "Read it after the baby is born. Aimee wants us to go home." I couldn't fight her anymore. Aimee yanked my hand and I looked at her. She looked at my mouth and I knew she wanted me to kiss her. I leaned forward and pressed my lips unto hers. I left it there for a few seconds and Aimee smiled when I pulled away. I waved and Nick and I walked out without looking back.

That was the last time I saw Aimee alive. Aimee had died after childbirth. Our baby girl, Quinn, was born at 4:31 a.m. and Aimee's heart stopped at 6:58 a.m. Mom had stayed back that night, and Rachel did too. Dad didn't sleep, and we all camped out in our living room. Nick and I fell asleep, my hand clutching the piece of paper that Aimee had written to me. I kept thinking about Aimee's face, how pale and frail she was. At around 7:15 a.m., Dad woke up and Nick up, and was crying. "You have a baby girl," he signed. "But Aimee died."

What kind of news is that? Good news and bad news at the same time. I didn't know how to react. Nick raised his hands to his head, and his eyes were red. Dad was staring at me, his eyes red as if he has been crying for some time. He let the news sink in, but I didn't know what to think. I just stood there, staring at Dad. Aimee was dead. I have a daughter. Aimee was dead. How can Aimee be dead? She's only nineteen years old! I knew what silence was. I haven't been able to hear my entire life. But for some reason, this was a different kind of silence. How is it that Aimee is dead? Dad kept staring at me, tears streaming from his face. Nick had then sat down and had his head in his hands. I sat down too and closed my eyes. I wanted to sleep.

"Do you want to go to the hospital right now? We can see the baby." Dad looked like he didn't even know where to start. I shook my head. That baby killed my girlfriend. I couldn't see her. "I thought the baby had a disability," I signed dully. My heart felt dead.

Dad nodded slowly. "Yes Simon, she does."

"Like Emma?"

Dad paused and signed. "Not exactly."

Even Nick had to look up at that. "What does the baby have?"

Dad fumbled near the phone and I saw he was looking for something. Then I saw him pick up a pad of paper where he had written it what the baby had. He couldn't read his writing, so I held out my hand and Dad put the paper in my hand.

"Cri du chat syndrome."

Nick looked over at me. "Cri du chat syndrome?" He looked thoughtful for a moment and signed. "In French, 'cri du chat'"—he sign-spelled cri du chat—"means 'cry of the cat.'"

Dad nodded and shrugged. "I have no idea what that means, the doctor tried to explain it to me on the phone, then my wife tried to, but to be honest there is so much going on right now."

Cry of the Cat?

I leaned back and closed my eyes. Too much was going on at once and I just wanted to close my eyes. Aimee is dead. I have a daughter who has a birth defect called "Cry of the Cat." I'm only eighteen years old, why is this all happening? Shouldn't I be out with friends, going to movies and clubs and having fun? When did all of this happen? I crawled into bed and closed my eyes. I knew I should go to the hospital, but I couldn't yet. I just wanted to sleep and have everything disappear for a while.

I opened my eyes and I signed this to Dad who looked like he understood. Nick and Dad exchanged words, I saw, and then Dad signed. "I am going to the hospital, and leaving Emma with the neighbor. Nick will stay here with you." I nodded and closed my eyes. I fell into a deep, dreamless sleep.

Chapter 14

I woke up late in the afternoon. As soon as I stood up, I felt a sharp pain in my head. Mom was sitting in the kitchen table drinking coffee and eating a bagel. Her eyes were red. I looked over at her and suddenly remembered everything that happened in the last twenty-four hours. Aimee's face. I am a Daddy. I have a daughter named Quinn. Quinn has a birth defect called "Cry of the Cat" in French. Mom looked over at me and put her bagel down. Mom looked like she shrunk since I last saw her. She stood up and walked over to me and signed. "Simon."

Seeing Mom's face suddenly made me cry and I went over to her and she wrapped her protective arms around me. I felt my legs give out and collapse to the ground and Mom followed me to the ground. I don't know how long she held me like that, but I just cried and cried and cried. Aimee was dead. How can Aimee be dead? She's only nineteen years old! There were so many things I wanted to ask Mom but I didn't want to let go of her hug. Mom rocked me back and forth. I could smell the hospital on her, as she was still wearing the same clothes. I took a deep breath and pulled back. I needed answers. I needed answers to cry to.

"What happened to Aimee, Mom? Why did she die?"

Mom shook her head and wiped the tears flowing from her eyes. "She lost too much blood and suffered a massive heart attack. Her heart was weak and the stress of the childbirth . . . ," Mom signed helplessly.

Something suddenly occurred to me. "Did she know that she was going to die?" I signed. "Is that why she asked me to go home?"

Mom shook her head. "She didn't know she was going to die. Or at least I don't think she knew. But we all knew something was wrong." Mom smiled me a watery smile. "You are a daddy. You have a beautiful baby girl. Aimee got to carry her for about ten minutes before they took her away. Aimee said you both decided to name her Quinn if it was a boy or a girl."

Mom stood up and went to her purse where she pulled out the family camera and showed me a picture of Aimee, very frail and pale, smiling as if it was the heaviest smile in the world and carrying a white bundle. For some reason, seeing the picture made me feel secure. Mom thought of getting a picture. At least I had some way of seeing her before she died. Mom smiled at me. "I knew you'd want one."

"But didn't Dad say that the baby had something French?" I signed. "Or was that a dream?"

Mom nodded. "Yes. The baby has a disability called cry of the cat syndrome. The doctor didn't explain too much yet as she knew we had so many other things to worry about." Mom stood up and pulled me off the floor and got me to sit on the kitchen table. There was a bag of bagels on the table and cream cheese. I helped myself to one. I was hungry. Next to the bagels were forms and pamphlets on "Facts on Cri du Chat Syndrome." About a stack of them.

"Coffee?" Mom signed. I nodded. I didn't like the taste of coffee too much, but it seemed to clear my head for some reason. I poured a few tablespoons of sugar.

"Simon, you need to eat. There are a lot of things we need to think and focus on right now. I know you're upset about Aimee, but Aimee told me to tell you that you need to be strong. And she told me to tell you to not forget to read the note she wrote you."

Oh right! The note! I reached into my jeans pocket and felt the paper inside. I was about to pull it out but then thought better of it.

Mom saw me pause. "Did you lose it?"

I shook my head. "I want to read it when I see Quinn." I pulled it out thought to make sure it was the right piece of paper, and it was. Nick had folded it into a square.

Nick. "Where is everyone?" I signed.

"Dad is at the hospital, and Nick took Rachel home. Rachel was holding Aimee's hand right up until her heart stopped. I was at nursery with Quinn." Mom looked exhausted.

"Where is Emma?"

"She's next door," Mom signed.

"I want to see Quinn. What are we going to do about Aimee's family?" I signed. This question brought a fresh new bout of tears in Mom's eyes.

"Dad called them and the number is out of service. I called Aimee's sister and the cell phone was also out of service. Rachel said she left a message to Aimee's cousin, but no one called back."

Wow. Aimee's family doesn't even know that she is dead?

Mom shook her head. "It doesn't seem like they even care." Mom stood up. "I just want to take a few hours' nap, and then we need to go by the hospital. Everyone understands the situation right now, it has been a terrible night, so they know that I went home to get you, but I just need to close my eyes for a bit." I nodded. Poor Mom. I hugged her.

"Thanks, Mom," I signed.

Mom smiled softly. "Congratulations, Simon. And my condolences." How ironic.

Chapter 15

I met my daughter that evening. Mom was more tired than she let on, and when she woke up, it was two hours before visiting hours were over. I had spent the day in my room, where Aimee had been staying, and found a few pictures of the both of us. Dad had been out all day, arranging funeral arrangements for Aimee. Nick and Rachel had helped. There was a support staff in the hospital that was helping Dad, and the funeral was to be three days from the day Quinn was born. When I arrived at the hospital, doctors and nurses extended their hands to send me my condolences. I didn't have any more tears in me, I couldn't cry anymore. There was nothing to cry. I was all cried out.

I was led to intensive care and with my heart pounding, I approached my little girl. She was in a respiratory thing, because she was having trouble breathing. Dad was standing off to the side, smiling faintly at me. I waved at him and he came over and gave me a huge hug. Mom had followed me in and saw her smile at the sight of Quinn. I let go of Dad and went over to my daughter. Her head was small, very small and she could fit into my one hand. She had an ID bracelet around her tiny feet. I didn't think she was pretty at all. She had a patch of hair and was darker than Aimee but lighter than me.

I leaned over and stared at her for a few moments. Then I saw her move. First her right foot shook and then her right hand. Then she opened her mouth. Mom came over to me and watched too. Quinn yawned, and then her tiny red face scrunched up. Then her bottom lip shook and I knew she was crying. Mom tapped me on the shoulder and signed. "Maybe that's why they call it cri du chat syndrome. She sounds like a cat when she cries."

The nurse who was standing nearby nodded with a small smile, and Mom interpreted her as she said, "Yes, that is why they call it cri du chat. They sound like they are meowing when they cry. It is due to the underdeveloped larynx" The nurses pointed to her throat. Quinn's eyes were shaped weirdly and she looked nothing like Aimee or me. I looked at the nurse, and then at Dad who seemed to understand what I was going to say.

"Yes, Simon, she's your daughter."

I didn't know what to think or what to feel. I remembered Aimee's note and pulled it out of my pocket. I unfolded it slowly. Aimee's writing made my body shake. She had written. "Be the best Daddy you can be. Please name the baby Quinn. I'm sorry I can't be there to watch you raise Quinn. Love, Aimee."

She knew.

Chapter 16

I met a social worker that evening. Her name was Lynn. There were tons of questions now on whether or not I was going to keep the baby. I felt so overwhelmed that evening that Dad and Mom told the doctors and nurses to please wait until the funeral was over. Right now, the baby was going to stay in the hospital because on top of having a disability, the baby was also jaundiced. Quinn had to stay under an ultraviolet light. The social worker knew everything about cri du chat and explained to us the best way she could without the technicalities of the doctors and nurses.

Every chance I got, I went to the bathroom, and Dad followed me, advising me to not lock the door. I just needed a few minutes to myself. Aimee wasn't buried yet, I had a daughter, she had a rare disability called "cri du chat," and I was only eighteen years old. The nurses gave me Aimee's bag that also had the journal in it, but I couldn't bring myself to read the journal yet. All of Aimee's clothes were inside, and also the bag with everything that Aimee would need for leaving the hospital.

I didn't go to school the next day, Dad called the principal saying that I would be out for the rest of the year. Mom couldn't argue. Both my parents knew exactly what I was going through. Mom took me to the hospital first thing in the morning and I watched as the nurses took care of Quinn. Mom did her best to interpret everything, but only had a few days of bereavement leave for work, so she asked the hospital if there could be a sign language interpreter for me. There was, and I met one lady named Manuella, a friendly woman who extended her condolences to me as soon as she saw me. She stayed with me and Mom that day, as I watched Quinn get changed, have tubes in her, and watch her cry.

Manuella signed. "Cri du chat syndrome is very rare."

Mom signed. "One in twenty thousand right?"

Manuella nodded. "Yes, and one in fifty thousand."

I shook my head in disbelief. Of course, Quinn had to be the one in fifty thousand. Of course she did.

Manuella looked at me. "You understand how Quinn got cri du chat syndrome right?"

I tilted my head back and forth to show that I wasn't quite sure. I frankly didn't care how she got it as I had already asked if there was a cure and the doctor who took care of Quinn said no. Manuella didn't ask me if I wanted to know; she just plunged right in. "Cri du chat syndrome is a deletion of a chromosome. It's that simple. The chromosome broke, in either your sperm or your girlfriend's egg, there is no way to find out, and when your girlfriend got pregnant, or when the egg got fertilized, then cri du chat syndrome developed."

Mom signed. "It is not hereditary, Simon."

I nodded. I didn't believe that, because either Aimee or I had to pass it down. So yes, it is hereditary and I made this statement to both Mom and Manuella. Mom looked stumped. Manuella looked impressed and signed to Mom. "Well, he does have a point."

We never got a hold of Aimee's family for the funeral. Rachel and Nick both did Aimee's eulogy and not even Aimee's cousin arrived, the one whom Rachel knew. Aimee's sister didn't show up, as we had no way of contacting them at all. All the numbers were not in service. Rachel and I went through Aimee's phone to call friends, but she had only nine numbers programmed into her phone. Her work, the retail store where she worked, Mom's cell, Dad's cell, my cell phone number, Nick's cell phone number, Aimee's cell phone number, her mom's home number (which was not in service) and her sister's cell phone number (which was also not in service).

It was then that I just realized I didn't meet any of Aimee's friends. I only knew Rachel, but Aimee didn't tell me of anyone else. It was a sad feeling, knowing that I didn't try harder to know anything about the mother of my daughter. We drove by Aimee's house, which was vacant and we didn't know. There was a "FOR SALE" sign on the front of the house and Dad suggested we go to the police to track down her mother so she can know that her daughter died. Mom was against it, signing that Aimee's mother clearly didn't want to be a part of Aimee's life.

Emma knew that Aimee had died, although she still kept asking when Aimee was coming over, so Mom decided to play along. The funeral was terrible. I cried the night before, staying at the hospital right up until I was told to leave the hospital. I just wanted to see Quinn. She was still very unattractive for a baby, but the nurses told me that she gained a pound. She now weighed 4.14 pounds. There were many things wrong with Quinn. Her brain was too small. She has cri du chat syndrome. We couldn't know more until Quinn gained a little more weight. Her larynx was underdeveloped, so every time she screwed her face up to cry, everyone at the hospital said that she sounded like a cat.

There were a lot of questions on how I was going to raise Quinn because I was deaf, and only eighteen years old. Mom and Dad were bombarded with questions too, and Manuella was there to interpret everything.

Mom and Rachel had gone shopping together to buy Aimee a dress for her casket. Mom and Dad paid for the entire funeral, and I was so angry at Aimee's family for not contacting us about Aimee at all. Rachel picked out a light blue dress, and we all met at the funeral home. Rachel was going to do her eulogy and Nick was going to sign beside her. The funeral was small. Nick's mother arrived too; it was the first time I met her, and she was a nice woman. She hugged me and signed. "Nick told me so much about you. I am so sorry about everything."

I knew that I would end up crying all throughout the funeral, so I refused to read Nick's interpretation of the eulogy. I sat next to my parents in the front and kept my eyes glued down. I turned around a few times hoping to see Aimee's family but there was hardly anyone at her funeral. Jeff, of course, showed up and made sure that the refreshments that were followed were on him. Jeff (with Dad's interpretation) told me to take some time off, and when I was ready to go back to work, I can. He also brought a huge pink teddy bear for "Baby Quinn."

I went up to her after the eulogy and kissed her forehead. She was prettier than when I last saw her. Her eyes were closed, but the undertaker had made her look very pretty. Her hair was all fluffed up. I had the journal both Aimee and I had written together for Quinn and tucked it into her casket. I also added a letter I had written while sitting next to Quinn in the Intensive Care Unit. It was one of the hardest letters I ever had to write and I was crying throughout the entire letter. I think finally, everything that I have been thinking of the last few days poured out into a letter that I knew Aimee would never read, but would somehow know.

> *"Dear Aimee,*
>
>   *I am writing this at the day of your funeral. I wanted you to know that Quinn is now 4.13 pounds. She's getting bigger. I don't know what happened to you, why you died, and every time someone tries to explain something to me, I just ignore them. I want to know, but I don't want to know. I'm angry that you didn't want me to be in the delivery room, but I understand why now. I do not know what to do with Quinn, as people want to take her away from me. I thought I could do this, with you here, but I am thinking of letting Children's Services take her from me. I know you wanted me to be the best dad ever, but I don't know if I can do this without you.*
>
>   *I do not know if the doctors told you, but the disability Quinn has is called cry of the cat in French. I can't hear her cry, but all the nurses and my parents say that she cries like a cat. She is a little bit ugly, but I hope she grows up to be as pretty as you. Aimee, I am sorry if I cannot keep our baby. These last few days have been terrible. Your mom's house is up for sale, and we tried to call her to come to the funeral, and she does not have a number anymore. We tried to call your sister too, but her number is not in service. I do not know how to contact them. All I had were those two numbers.*
>
>   *My parents have been helping me every way, but I can't do this. They are also getting older, and they still have Emma. I haven't gone back to school since you died. I thought I can do this without you, but I can't. Why did you die? Why did you leave me? I cannot take care of Quinn by myself. I want to but I can't. I am too young, and I can't even hear her cry, how am I supposed to know if she needs to eat? I wanted to do this, but so much has changed since our decision. Please do not be mad at me. I am only eighteen years old. I am scared to take care of someone whom I cannot even hear.*
>
>   *The doctors told me so many things can go wrong with Quinn. Her body may not grow properly, and she can also be deaf. Her speech will be "impaired." They also said that she will have severe mental disability growing up, and it is just too*

much for me to take on. She isn't like Emma. The only thing I can offer to Quinn is the fact that I can sign to her. I am so sorry, Aimee. I wish I were able to take care of her. I cannot do this by myself. I am too young. Even if you were still alive, we would still need my parents. But without you, I can't do this. I wanted to write this letter to you so you know what is going to happen. I know you can't read this, but I need you to know what is going to happen to our daughter. I do not know if she will be adopted, or if the government will take her, but they have already spoken to my parents, and my parents left the decision on me. It was so hard to see them so tired. They still have Emma to take care of, and Quinn in the picture will just be too hard on them. I know if you are alive you will be okay with this, but I don't know what happened.

I am sorry, Aimee. I will let you know what I am going to do in a few days. We are burying you today, and then tomorrow we will have an appointment with a social worker named Lynn who was sent to help us with Quinn.

I love you and I wish we could have had more time together.

Simon

I had tucked this letter inside Aimee's casket knowing that wherever she was, she would be reading it.

We buried Aimee that afternoon, in the fresh October weather, on the tenth of October, three days after Quinn was born.

The next day, I carried Quinn for the first time. She had gained another pound. I didn't move when I was carrying her, I was so afraid to break her. She was so tiny, it didn't even feel like anything was in my hands. Mom and Dad and Emma came with me, and we took pictures of Quinn. She still looked rather disgusting for a baby, but Mom signed that most babies don't look cute until they gain a little bit of weight. Quinn's eyes were always squeezed shut, but the shape of them reminded me of a cat. Or maybe that was just because of the name of her disability. Manuella was there to help interpret things. I was allowed to see Quinn for two more days after this, and then the government will take her from me.

"Are you sure you are okay with this?" Dad signed to me when we were given some privacy. I thought back to how much my life had changed in the last year, in the past week, and nodded. I needed to properly grieve Aimee, and I knew deep down that throwing myself into caring for a child that I am not ready to raise is the worst way to go. That would be so selfish of me. Especially with a baby who was born with a disability as severe as cri du chat syndrome. Aimee's death had left a huge whole in my heart. I collapsed in tears when Aimee's casket was lowered six feet into the ground. I cried when they closed to casket, and we all said our final goodbyes. I had copied the letter I had written to Aimee in my journal as that was the one thing that got me through the last few weeks. I jotted everything I could when I had the chance and copied the letter so I knew exactly what I said to Aimee. Aimee was the first woman I had ever fallen in love with, and now she is gone. I can't raise Quinn under the circumstances. I just can't.

"You know that whatever you decide, Si, we are here for you, right?" Mom signed. I nodded.

"If that is your final decision, we will sign all of the papers tomorrow," Dad signed to me. I nodded. I looked at Emma who grinned at me. My little sister has held my hand throughout this whole ordeal, sleeping with me every chance she could, holding my hand and just sitting beside me. I looked at how pretty her smile was and then looked down at Quinn. She was asleep, her chest heaving in and out. She wasn't under the ultraviolet rays anymore, but I noticed that she a tiny birthmark on the left side of her body. Just like mine! I pointed this out to Mom, by trying to nod my head toward the birthmark. She followed my eyes and saw the birthmark and grinned. "So she is definitely your child," Mom signed.

Nick and Rachel came by an hour later, and Mom told them of my decision. Nick nodded and Rachel smiled at me.

"It's a good decision," Rachel said, while Nick interpreted. "Aimee wants you to be happy."

I said my last farewells to Quinn the next day. She had gained another pound, and her eyes were still squeezed shut, as if to keep all the light from coming into her life. I was not allowed to hold her by myself, as a nurse stood by. Manuella and my parents were in the other room as I told my parents they can tell the hospital and the social worker Lynn that I was going to allow the government to take Quinn from me. I was told that I needed to respect her upbringing and not contact Quinn and allow her to contact me when she reaches the age of eighteen. I don't know where I will be by the time I turn thirty-six, but I can only hope that Quinn does find a way to reach me. If not, then it wasn't meant to be. I didn't want to know who was going to be watching her. Children's Aid Services would take Quinn away from me, and from there, that was it. I couldn't find out anything about Quinn, and it was only her decision whether or not she wanted to find me.

"Do you want the baby to have access to knowing who you are?" Manuella signed to me when all four of them were back into the room. I looked at Mom and Dad, who nodded at me encouragingly. I nodded. "Yes." Lynn smiled at me. "It's going to be tough, but you know that we offer services to deal with the ideas of giving your child up for adoption."

I wanted to sign, but my arms were full. Mom laughed and took Quinn from me.

"It's okay. I have my family," I signed to Lynn and Manuella. I raised my arms back to my mom who gave me Quinn, and I kissed her on her forehead.

"Do you want five more minutes with her?" Dad signed. I nodded. Even the nurse smiled and walked out of the room with everyone. I was finally completely alone with my daughter. I couldn't sign to her, so I spoke to her through my thoughts.

"Quinn, grow big and strong. Find me one day. There's only two of us out there. Look for me." And with that I kissed her on her forehead again. This time though, Quinn opened her eyes. I had never seen her eyes, and they were a weird-looking color. Dark brown with green specks. She looked right at me and then screwed her face up again. I don't know how a cat meows, but I imagined it was a pretty sound. I imitated her face. In ten minutes, she was taken from me. For good.

Chapter 17

I went to Aimee's gravesite every day until it was too sad to endure. I sat down on the slightly wet and soggy ground and wrote to her in my journals. I wrote about everything, how I was feeling, how much I missed her, and how Quinn had looked up at me and I got to see the color of her eyes. One day when I was sitting on the ground, just finishing up some thoughts on paper, I felt someone touch my shoulder. I turned around and saw a woman.

Aimee's mom.

She had a cigarette in her hand, and she had lost a lot of weight. I looked at her, stunned. She was also carrying a single yellow flower. I stood up and let her talk to Aimee. I know it was rude to sit and stare, but I watched as Aimee's mother knelt in front of her gravesite and bent her head down. I saw her lips moving, but I didn't dare interpret it. Finally, she stopped and noticed I was still there. She smiled at me, and I wasn't scared of her anymore. I came over to her and shook her hand. She shook it back and then pulled me in to hug her. I was surprised. She started to talk and then stopped herself, blushing. I grinned and handed her a pen and opened to a fresh page in the notebook.

"Was she happy?" she wrote and handed it back to me. I read it and grinned. "Very," I wrote back.

"Was the baby a boy or a girl?" Aimee's mom wrote.

"A girl," I wrote back.

"What was her name?" I was surprised that Aimee's mom wrote in the past tense. She must have known what happened to Quinn. I wasn't going to question it. It was none of my business.

"Quinn," I wrote, smiling, and passed the notebook back to her. Aimee's mom gasped, and she covered her mouth with her hand. Tears fell from her eyes, and I cocked my head to the side. I just looked at her. Maybe she liked the name too. Aimee's mom regained her composure and waved her hand in front of her face. She wiped her eyes. Wow, Aimee's mom must really like the name. Aimee's mom smiled shakily at me and wrote, "That's my name. My name is Quinn."

I was stunned. Aimee never told me that. She was the one who suggested the name, and I went along with it because it was perfect for both a girl and a boy. I had no idea she named the baby after her mom. Even after the way she treated her. Quinn and I stood in front of each other for a few minutes, and then Aimee's mom held her hand out for the notebook. She wrote, "I come here every day, and you are always here writing. What are you writing?"

I grinned at her and wrote, "I am writing my first book. One day I am going to get it published."

Quinn wrote, "What's it called?" and handed the book back to me. I wrote the title of the book that I have been working on for the last few months.

Simon Says.

CPSIA information can be obtained at www.ICGtesting.com
Printed in the USA
LVOW062130191011

251257LV00001B/1/P